FOX IN THE FROST

Mrs. Ponsonby got out of her car and began to protest. "Mr. Western, what on earth is happening? My Fox Watch scheme is only meant to drive the foxes out of Welford. I didn't intend for you to come out and shoot them!"

The men ignored her. Her wailing voice was lost in the wind.

There was a sharp crack, then another and another. Puffs of smoke rose in the air as the guns went off. *Bang! Bang! Bang!* Mandy felt her heart jolt and shudder.

James came to a halt, his face suddenly white. He turned and stared at Mandy.

With stiff, leaden legs, James and Mandy forced themselves to follow, dreading what they would find when they crested the hill.

"You were right." James reached the top and stared down. "We were too late."

Give someone you love a home!
Read about the animals of Animal Ark™

FOX in the FROST

Ben M. Baglio

Illustrations by Jenny Gregory

Cover illustration by
Mary Ann Lasher

AN
APPLE
PAPERBACK

SCHOLASTIC INC.
New York Toronto London Auckland Sydney
Mexico City New Delhi Hong Kong

ISBN 0-439-23017-9

All rights reserved. Published by Scholastic Inc., 555 Broadway, New York, NY 10012, by arrangement with Working Partners Limited. ANIMAL ARK is a trademark of Working Partners Limited. SCHOLASTIC, APPLE PAPERBACKS, and associated logos are trademarks and/or registered trademarks of Scholastic Inc.

12 11 10 9 8 .   3 4 5/0

Printed in the U.S.A.   40
First Scholastic printing, November 2000

Special thanks to Jenny Oldfield
Thanks also to C. J. Hall,
B.Vet.Med., M.R.C.V.S., for reviewing
the veterinary material contained in this book.

™

One

"Blackie, come back here!" James Hunter shouted. The black Labrador ignored him.

"That's a very obedient dog you have there." Mandy Hope grinned. She clipped a sprig of holly from a thick bush by the roadside. They were out in the field, close to the Beacon, gathering holly for Christmas. The hillside was covered in white frost that sparkled in the sun.

"Blackie!" James jumped over a gate and careered after him, down the path to High Cross Farm.

"So well-trained, so reliable!"

"Yeah, yeah!" James's voice carried on the wind, before he vanished between the high stone walls.

Mandy reached higher. There was a sprig laden with shiny red berries. It would look great over the doorway at Animal Ark. She wanted the waiting room to be bright and cheerful in the days before the festive season. But she reached too far. Her fingertips missed the branch and the frosty ground was slippery. "Aagh!" Her arms whirled and she tipped forward.

Blackie heard her cry and came galloping back across the field.

"Blackie, where are you?" James's faint voice called.

"He's here!" Mandy was in the ditch. The dog's black nose snuffled her cheek. He butted her and licked the frost from her face. "Ouch!" She gave up trying to fend him off. "Ouch! Ouch!"

"What are you doing down there?" James peered over the wall, his face red from running.

"Ouch! These holly leaves are sharp!" Mandy's hat fell over her eyes as Blackie wrestled with her. "Get him off me, James. I'm getting prickled to death!"

"Here, boy!" It was James's turn to grin. He climbed the wall and tried to tug the dog away. "Sorry, Mandy, he thinks you want to play!"

"Well, I don't. Ouch! Get off, Blackie!" At last Mandy

struggled to her feet. The seat of her trousers was covered in frost and dead holly leaves. Her hat finally fell to the ground as she bent to brush herself off.

Another game! Blackie seized the red woolen hat and charged up the hill toward Upper Welford Hall.

Mandy groaned. "Okay, I know it serves me right for being rude about him." She sighed.

"Come on, we'd better get him back before he decides to invade the Hall gardens." James set off after Blackie.

"Yep, Mr. Western would really love that!" The owner of Upper Welford Hall would be furious with anyone who even so much as touched his smooth lawns and perfect flowerbeds. Christmas or no Christmas, he would be phoning their moms and dads — if not the police — to complain.

"Uh-oh, I've lost him." James came to a halt by the big double gates. "Did you see which way he went?"

Mandy stumbled into James. "No!" she gasped. She turned full circle, taking in the sweep of the white hillside, the tiny houses of Welford nestled in the valley, the shining river as it snaked its way through. "But he can't have disappeared!"

James bent to peer under a hedge. "Blackie!" he whispered. "Look, Mandy, there's your hat!" He crawled along the hedge bottom and reached out for it. When he stood up, he looked worried. "His footprints go right across the lawn!"

"Where to?" Mandy stared at the blank windows and closed doors of the lovely old hall. She prayed that Mr. Western was out.

"I can't see. Wait, what was that?"

They heard an odd noise, somewhere between a squawk and a cackle. It was the annoyed alarm call of a bird. "It sounds like Blackie's found something else to chase."

This time James groaned. "Pheasants!"

They watched as a pair of russet-brown birds scuttled out of the opposite hedge and across Mr. Western's flowerbeds. Their dark heads gleamed and their long tail feathers skimmed the frosty earth.

"Oh, Blackie!" Mandy was disappointed in him. James's dog was lively, but usually not so much trouble. Now the birds broke into a run and began to flap their wings. They clattered and whirred as they took flight.

"*Woof!*" Blackie came up from behind and sidled between James and Mandy.

Mandy stared at James. "What set the birds off if it wasn't Blackie after all?"

"Search me!" James looked all around the huge garden for the culprits, but saw nothing.

The pheasants made a great din as they flew off. A door in the house flew open and Mr. Western strode out. "Foxes!" he cried. "Dennis, a couple of foxes are after the pheasants!" He called his farm manager out of the house after him. "Pests! Vermin! Let's get after them as quick as we can!"

By this time, James had a tight hold on Blackie's collar. He didn't want him getting in the line of fire as the two men came out with their shotguns.

"How do they know it's foxes?" Mandy breathed. She crouched beside James and Blackie in the shelter of the hedge, watching the heavy birds fly overhead.

"Look!" James had seen them at last.

Two foxes swerved across the lawn toward them. Ears pricked, amber eyes gleaming, they ran silently and swiftly across the frost-covered grass.

"*That* was the trail we saw!" James whispered. "Not Blackie!"

"Shh!" Mandy longed for the foxes to reach the safety of the hedge before Mr. Western and Dennis Saville spotted them. She wouldn't want to see any creature harmed by a gun. And the two foxes were beautiful. Their coats were red and silky smooth. Their chests and bellies were white, their ears and legs black. They carried their magnificent bushy tails low to the ground. But it was their eyes, a bright, shining amber, edged with black, that fascinated Mandy. The foxes ran side by side, deprived of their prey, for by now the birds were long gone.

Blackie gave a deep, rumbling growl. James held tight. "I think they'll make it!" he whispered.

The foxes had reached the edge of the lawn. Silent as shadows they came, slinking into the hedge a few yards from where James, Mandy, and Blackie hid.

"Over there!" Sam Western spotted the fresh tracks. He heard the movement of animals brushing against undergrowth, of twigs snapping underfoot. He raised his gun to his shoulder and aimed it at the hedge.

"Don't shoot!" Mandy stood up. It was time to show themselves. If they distracted the men's attention, the foxes would be able to slide off unnoticed. She felt James stand beside her, heard Blackie bark, then saw a red flash of fox out of the corner of her eye. The pair were off, through the hedge, up the open hillside toward the Beacon.

"What on earth . . . ?" Mr. Western lowered his gun. "Is that you, Mandy Hope?"

She stepped into view between the wide iron gates. "Yes. We're collecting holly for our Christmas decorations." Her voice held steady, though her legs trembled. It had been a close call for the two foxes.

"Collecting holly?" He strode down the drive. "Look here, you nearly got yourselves shot. We're after a couple of foxes. Did you see them? Which way did they go?" Flinging open the gate, Sam Western waited for Mandy's reply.

Mandy swallowed hard. With a warning glance at James, she waved her arm toward the valley. "I think they headed that way."

She sent the two men hurrying off in the wrong direction, boots crunching over the frost, breathing clouds of steam into the cold, crisp air.

"Oh, Dr. Adam, whatever is wrong with poor Toby?" Mrs. Ponsonby sailed into the crowded waiting room at Animal Ark, her mongrel dog tucked under her arm. Her broad face was red and she was out of breath as she pushed past other patients waiting quietly in the room. "Excuse me, but this is an emergency. Poor Toby can hardly breathe. He needs to see a vet immediately!"

Adam Hope came out from behind the reception desk and guided her straight into a treatment room. He beckoned Mandy to follow. "Jean, could you put my appointments back by ten minutes, please?" he called to the receptionist, who began to fend off the grumbles and complaints of the other pet owners in the waiting room.

Mandy went in and closed the door after them. She watched her dad begin to examine the dog.

"He's certainly breathing heavily. He hasn't been left in a room that's much too warm, without any ventilation, by any chance?" Dr. Adam placed his stethoscope on Toby's chest.

"Of course not. Oh, it's a heart attack, isn't it? How dreadful. Is it the excitement of Christmas, Dr. Adam?

Toby loves Christmas, but he does tend to get over-excited. Oh dear, it is; it's his heart. I knew it!"

Toby stood on the treatment table panting heavily.

"No, I don't think so, Mrs. Ponsonby. Toby's heart sounds fine. Now, there's no discharge from the eyes or the nose, as far as I can tell."

Mrs. Ponsonby still feared the worst. "Oh, it's distemper, isn't it?"

Mandy's dad shook his head.

"Pneumonia, then?"

"No, his lungs are fine, too." Dr. Adam stood back to scratch his chin. "How long has Toby been like this?"

"Ten whole minutes! I popped into the post office to see Mrs. McFarlane. I left my precious Toby and Pandora outside, and when I came out, there he was, in this terrible state. I was convinced he was about to breathe his last, so I rushed him straight here in the car."

"Hmm. Well, he seems to be improving now."

Mandy agreed. The scruffy mongrel was already wagging his tail. His little black nose was moist, his eyes bright. Certainly there didn't seem to be much wrong with him now.

"Tell me, Mrs. Ponsonby, was there anybody else around when you came out of the post office? Anyone with a dog, for instance?"

The large, fussy woman paused to consider. "So you think Toby might have caught something infectious from another dog? Well, let's see now. Yes, the new people from the Old Vicarage were close by. Mr. and Mrs. Dixon, isn't it? And they had their brute with them. Of course, that must be it!" She bristled and shook with outrage at the idea.

"Their brute?" Dr. Hope was puzzled.

"A collie," Mandy explained. She knew the Dixon family had moved into the large old house with their dog and her litter of five pups.

"Great big nasty woolly thing. All that shaggy fur; so unhygienic. No wonder Toby's caught something unpleasant!"

"Maybe, maybe not!"

Mandy saw a flicker of a smile at the corners of her father's mouth.

"Is this dog a 'she'?" he asked.

"To be sure. Henrietta. Such a silly name for a rough brute like that. Yes, a female."

"Hmm."

Mandy could see from her father's hesitation that he didn't know how to break the news. She felt her own mouth begin to quiver.

"Well, er, Mrs. Ponsonby, I don't think there's anything seriously the matter with Toby. Look, you can see he's already beginning to calm down nicely."

"Nothing the matter? But this is an emergency!"

"No, luckily you were mistaken." He glanced at Mandy and took a deep breath. "The fact is, Mrs. Ponsonby, Toby was just a little overexcited, shall we say. Let's put it down to the fact that he must have fallen prey to the lovely Henrietta's charms."

Mandy put one hand to her mouth and coughed. In a flurry of sudden activity, she began to tidy a shelf in a corner of the room.

"Fallen prey . . . ?" Mrs. Ponsonby blushed bright red to the roots of her blue-rinsed hair. "Oh, I see. You mean he was attracted to a member of the opposite sex? Oh, my! Oh, dear." She frowned and huffed, then hurried forward to scoop Toby into her arms. "You're sure, now, Dr. Adam? You don't think we need a second opinion from Dr. Emily?"

Mandy's mom was hard at work in the treatment room next door. Mandy had shown Ernie Bell in there with his young cat, Twinkie.

"Quite sure." Adam Hope was firm. "I think you should take Toby home, give him a nice cool drink, and let him have a nap. He'll be right as rain after that, you'll see."

"Yes, I'm sure you're right. Come along, Toby." Mrs. Ponsonby couldn't leave fast enough. "It's so good of you to see us so promptly, Adam. But now we mustn't take up any more of your valuable time!"

Mandy watched her rush out in a wave of sweet perfume. "Whoo-oo, *Adam!*" she teased her dad.

But already Jean, the receptionist, was showing the next patient in, and they soon forgot about Mrs. Ponsonby and lovelorn Toby. There was a spaniel with a swollen earflap, and a budgie who was going bald. Then there was a litter of kittens for Mandy to feed and clean in the residential unit, and a dozen other jobs to keep her busy until supper. Afterward, she was hoping to go with her mother to the Old Vicarage, where, with a bit of luck, she would meet the gorgeous Henrietta!

Two

"Hi, Mandy, need any help putting up the decorations?"

At four o'clock James stopped in to see her. He'd taken Blackie home after their adventure at Upper Welford Hall, but now he was back. The waiting room was emptying out, and Mandy was busy tying bunches of holly together with string, ready to hang over the doors.

"Hi, James. Yes, great." After the holly, they could hang silver streamers. She explained her ideas and they set about making the room look as Christmasy as possible.

"You don't think you're going a little bit over the top?"

Jean asked, as James and Mandy pinned the streamers from corner to corner and hung holly from every shelf and cornice. She checked off the last patients and got ready to leave.

"Why not? Isn't that what Christmas is all about?" Simon, the Animal Ark nurse, came out of a treatment room and nodded his approval. "It looks great!"

"Thanks." James climbed down from a stool and stood back to admire their efforts.

"Will you be going to the grand ceremony on Friday?" Simon asked Jean. "You know, the big occasion!"

The receptionist sniffed. "I'm not sure. I think I'd rather have our usual carol service outside the Fox and Goose."

"Oh, come on, Jean, it'll be a nice change." Simon was young and ready to move with the times. "How often do we get the chance to see a famous soap star in the flesh?"

Mandy pricked up her ears. "What famous soap star?" This was the first she'd heard of it. Normally at Christmas, everyone in Welford got together to sing and have a party in the village hall.

"You know, Joe Wortley from *Dale End*. He's coming to turn on the Christmas lights. Haven't you heard?"

"Not *the* Joe Wortley?" Mandy's eyes lit up. She

watched the popular television series whenever she could. Joe Wortley played the young, good-looking doctor, Justin Scott.

From behind her desk Jean tutted. "What's wrong with good old Father Christmas? Some of us prefer the tried and tested ways, Simon. Ask any of the old-timers around here."

But Mandy was getting carried away. "It sounds great! Whose idea was it?" She rolled up the ball of string and put the scissors back behind the desk.

"The Dixons, I think. They're personal friends of Joe Wortley and they invited him to Welford for Christmas. They asked him to turn on the lights as a special favor. He isn't even going to charge for appearing."

"I'll be there!" James was excited, too. "What time does it begin?"

"Seven-thirty, outside the pub." Simon turned back to Jean. "There'll be carols as well, you know. Why don't you come?"

"I might."

"Come on. Just because the Dixons are new to the village isn't a good reason to snub them. They didn't intend to upset anyone."

"No, but they should have consulted with the Christmas committee first." Jean was a member of the committee, along with Ernie Bell, Mrs. Ponsonby, and Mandy's grandmother. "I call it very high-handed."

"Well, maybe. But staying away isn't the answer. Everyone else is going to be there, you know."

It would be a hard job to convince Jean, Mandy realized. For herself, she was too thrilled about Joe Wortley to take much notice. "He's my favorite actor in the whole show!" she told James. "And, just think, he's going to be in Welford this coming Friday!"

". . . All that fuss," Jean grumbled quietly in the background. "Just think of the money that's been spent on those lights."

"I'm going to get his autograph!" James vowed.

"Me, too!" Mandy could hardly wait.

". . . The Dixons, the Parker Smythes; these wealthy families, they're all the same . . ." Jean sighed.

"Maybe he'll bring some other actors from *Dale End* with him, too!" Mandy pictured a whole host of television stars.

". . . More money than sense," Jean said, snapping the appointment book closed and buttoning up her coat.

Mandy was still bubbling with excitement when she drove with her mom and James into the village after office hours had ended.

"Did I tell you we saw two foxes up near the Beacon?" she asked Dr. Emily, as they swept past the post office. The village street lamps glowed, and all the houses were lit up as people arrived home from work.

"Three times," Dr. Emily reminded her with a smile. "And in broad daylight, too. That's unusual. They're pretty secretive creatures as a rule."

"Why don't farmers like them?" James asked. They hadn't told anyone about Mr. Western's hasty call for his gun as soon as he'd spotted the intruders on his lawn. Mandy and he thought it best not to mention how close they'd come to peering down the wrong end of the barrel. "I mean, I know they're supposed to kill chickens. But it's up to the farmers to make sure their hens are safely locked up at night, isn't it?"

"It depends on how you look at it." Dr. Emily drove through the village to drop James off before she and Mandy doubled back to call in on vets' business at the Old Vicarage. "Like most things. Some people see foxes as pests because they seem to kill without reason. Even if they're not hungry, they'll slaughter a whole coop full of chickens. They even say a fox will kill a young lamb, though I've never seen that myself."

"I think they just blame foxes because they have to blame someone." Mandy sprang to the animals' defense. "They call them cunning, but that just means clever, really. They're cleverer than a lot of people, come to think of it!"

"Maybe." The car pulled up at James's gate and Dr. Emily let him out. "As a matter of fact, foxes aren't such a serious threat to farmers. They mostly hunt voles and other small mammals. They eat fruit and beetles, grass, cereals; anything they can get hold of. They're especially partial to earthworms, actually!"

"And the contents of our garbage!" James added. "My mom keeps saying we've got foxes in our yard."

"She's probably right. There are a lot of urban foxes around now. It's easier for them to find food in towns and villages than in the open countryside."

"I wish we had them in *our* yard," Mandy said. "I'd love to see them out of my bedroom window first thing in the morning!"

"Try putting out a plateful of worms then!" James grinned and said good-bye. "Good luck at the vicarage."

Mandy and Dr. Emily were going to meet the Dixons for the first time. Mrs. Dixon had called Animal Ark and arranged a home visit. She said that the five collie pups needed their second round of vaccinations. So Mandy and her mom said good-bye to James and drove back to the center of the village.

The Old Vicarage stood out of sight behind the

church on big grounds that rolled down to the river's edge. The house was enormous. It was built of stone, with strong pillars at the top of a flight of wide steps leading up to the main door. Inside, Mandy glimpsed bright chandeliers, polished floors, and dark red, patterned carpets. She followed her mother, smoothing her blond hair and tugging at the hem of her sweater. Somehow, a house like this made her nervous.

A girl of about her own age answered the door. She was tall and skinny, with jet-black hair worn in straight bangs and falling like curtains on either side of her pale face. Her eyes were light gray, her mouth unsmiling.

"Hello, we've come to give the puppies their shots," Dr. Emily said pleasantly, introducing herself and Mandy.

The girl sniffed and led them across the hall. "Mommy!" she yelled up the curving staircase. "It's the vet!" Then she disappeared into a room where music blared and a television screen flickered.

A woman came down to greet them. "I'm Helena Dixon. You must be Emily Hope. The pups are in the utility room at the back of the house. It's quite warm in there, and it means they're out of the way, not getting under everyone's feet, you know." She smiled and bustled ahead. Like her daughter, she was slim and dark.

She wore red lipstick and gold earrings, and her nails were painted the same shade of red as her lips, Mandy noticed.

"You say the pups are twelve weeks old?" Emily Hope asked quietly. "And they had their first round of shots before you came to Welford?"

"That's right. The little rascals; I'd no idea collie pups got into so much mischief. That's why we keep them out there, otherwise our poor furniture wouldn't be fit to be seen."

Mrs. Dixon took them through the kitchen and out into a bare room lined with a washing machine, dryer, and freezer. "Of course, it's different with Henrietta. She was fully house-trained when we got her. She's in with Sophie watching *Dale End* on TV. But as for the pups, the sooner they go off to good homes the better!" she exclaimed as she switched on the light.

"Oh!" Mandy couldn't stop herself from crying out in delight as five furry little bundles hurtled toward them. They were a mixture of black, brown, and white; tiny, shaggy miniatures, some with black patches over one eye, some with white paws, some with brown paws, and all with shiny button noses and pink tongues that lolled and panted as they leaped and tumbled to the floor.

"You see what I mean?" Helena Dixon stepped back

out of their way. "I can't wear a decent pair of trousers with these puppies jumping up all the time."

Dr. Emily put her bag on the floor and took off her jacket. "Okay, now I'm going to give them each a shot for distemper, hepatitis, and parvovirus. You haven't found a problem with any of the pups so far?"

Mrs. Dixon frowned, then shrugged.

"I mean, are they all fit and healthy? They're all equally active?"

"Much too active, if you ask me."

Dr. Emily asked Mandy to hold the first pup as she prepared a syringe. "They certainly look lively enough."

The four other little bundles of fur skidded and flung themselves at Mandy and Dr. Emily. One in particular charged without looking where he was going. He crashed into a chair leg and rolled over.

"That's Nipper," Mrs. Dixon said with a sigh. "So called because he nips about all over the place. And that one you're holding is Flora. That's Daisy, that's Henry, and that's Olivia." She named them each in turn. Flora yelped as Dr. Emily gave her the shot. Mandy stroked her, then let her go.

"Number two!" Out came the second syringe. Dr. Emily asked Mandy to move on to Daisy. "You're making sure to worm them?" she said to Helena Dixon.

"My daughter, Sophie, does that. You met her when

you arrived. But yes, I'm quite sure that side is taken care of." The puppies' owner sidestepped another frantic charge. "Listen, you don't mind if I leave you to it, do you? We have a guest arriving for dinner." She began to back out of the utility room into the kitchen.

"No, of course not. Mandy and I can manage here." Dr. Emily smiled and carried on with her work. "We'll see ourselves out."

Obviously glad to escape, Helena Dixon closed the door behind her.

Only then did Mandy relax. She played with the pups while her mom checked their paws, ears, eyes, and throats. Mandy tickled them and rubbed their tummies, made them squirm and wriggle with pleasure. Henry jumped into her lap as she sat cross-legged on the tiled floor, and Olivia yelped to be picked up. Daisy and Flora rolled on their backs and waved their legs in the air, while Nipper charged and bumped straight into Dr. Emily's bag.

"Oops!" Mandy laughed as her mom set him back on his feet. Nipper shook himself and charged on.

"Come on, we're all finished here." Dr. Emily watched his wobbly course. "Time to go!"

Reluctantly, Mandy stood up and made sure that the pups were all safely inside the room, then she followed her mom quickly to the door and turned out the light.

Together they slipped out of the kitchen, leaving behind the sound of high yelps and little paws scrabbling on the bare floor in the dark utility room.

Out in the hall, Mandy noticed the television still on in the room where Sophie had been. The door stood ajar, but there was no sign of Henrietta or of Sophie herself. *At least she could have shown some interest in the puppies*, Mandy thought.

She didn't like what she'd seen so far of the newcomers to the village. For all their money and their famous friend, neither Sophie nor her mother had struck her as particularly happy. In fact, they seemed cool and stand-offish.

And anyone who can lock puppies up in a boring, bare utility room doesn't deserve to keep them! Mandy thought.

She headed across the richly patterned rug in the hallway, grumbling to herself, following her mother toward the big main door.

Suddenly, the doorbell rang and stopped them in their tracks. The television went off and Sophie shot out into the hall. Mrs. Dixon came running downstairs, newly changed into a tight black dress and high-heeled shoes. Her husband strode out of yet another room. They all made for the door at once.

Mandy and Dr. Emily stepped aside quickly as Sophie

reached the door first. She pulled it open, and in stepped . . . yes! Mandy's mouth fell open. She managed to clamp it shut again just in time. In stepped Joe Wortley himself!

"Joe, darling, how nice to see you!" Helena Dixon drew him into the warm house.

The actor kissed and embraced the two female Dixons and shook hands with Mr. Dixon. He was just how he looked on television; the same handsome face with its square jaw and gray eyes, the fair hair. *But he's not as tall as he looks on TV*, Mandy thought with a tiny glimmer of disappointment.

"Come in, come in." Mr. Dixon was all smiles. "We're glad you could make it."

"I came straight here from filming in Walton," Joe said. He flashed an absentminded smile in the direction of Mandy and her mom.

His voice was as deep and kind as it was when he played Dr. Justin Scott, Mandy thought. It struck her that she was actually in the same room as Joe Wortley, and she felt her heart begin to race. He did look a bit older in real life. She studied the wrinkles at the corners of his eyes, the sagging flesh under his chin. Still, she didn't mind.

"Come on, Mandy." Dr. Emily was trying to slide out of the door. She succeeded in pulling Mandy after her.

"Who was that?" they heard the great man say, as Sophie closed the door after them.

"Only the vet," Helena Dixon explained. "Oh, Joe, you haven't seen our gorgeous little collie pups, have you? You must come and look at them now, right this minute, before we do anything else! Wait and see, they're absolutely adorable!"

Mandy floated down the steps. Her feet crunched on the gravel drive. She waited under the starlit sky as her mom unlocked the car door. *Joe Wortley! Just wait until I tell everyone I've actually seen him in real life!*

"Hop in, Mandy. Are you okay?" Dr. Emily started the engine.

She nodded. "Isn't he ... wonderful, Mom?" She couldn't think of any other word to describe him.

"Hmm, I suppose so, if you like that sort of thing." They rode off out of the grounds, past the church, back into the village. The lights of the Fox and Goose glowed warmly. The pub was busy, the parking lot crowded.

Mandy made out the outline of a tall Christmas tree and strings of lights decorating the yard and the pub itself; all waiting to be turned on by Joe Wortley this coming Friday. "Didn't you like him?" she breathed, turning to her mom.

"What? Yes, I expect he's very charming." Dr. Emily's

mind was on something else as she turned into the lane leading to Animal Ark.

"What are you thinking about?" Mandy wondered if it had something to do with the Dixons' puppies; something that her mom hadn't mentioned when they were in the house. "There's nothing wrong, is there?"

"No, no, I'm probably worrying about nothing."

Animal Ark was in sight; the familiar wooden sign, the cozy old house, and the clinic at the back. "Sure?" If there was a problem, Mandy would rather know.

"Yes, I was just thinking about little Nipper. I wonder why he doesn't look where he's going. But it's probably just that he's got too much energy, like most puppies of his age. It's nothing. Come on, let's go and see what your dad's been up to while we've been out!"

Three

". . . Putting up the Christmas tree, that's what I've been up to!" Dr. Adam cried. "And now I'm covered from head to toe in pine needles."

Mandy brushed him off. "Can we decorate it right away?" she asked. Once the tree was up in the big cottage kitchen, it really felt like Christmas.

So they called Grandma and Grandpa Hope over from Lilac Cottage, and together the whole family hung silver baubles, ribbons, and lights on the tree.

"More tea?" Grandma was in charge of the teapot. She came around with refills, and a plate of warm cookies.

"Please." Dr. Adam stood on a stool, trying to place the angel on the top of the tree.

"Yes, please." Mandy's grandpa plugged in the lights. "Hey, presto!" he said as he turned on the switch. The lights winked prettily.

"Ooh, yes, I'd love another cup!" Dr. Emily carried presents to put under the tree. They were shiny and bright; big boxes, small squashy parcels, round things, and long, thin, mysterious things.

Mandy was trying to guess what each present might be when the telephone rang. "I'll get it!" She raced to answer.

"Hello, Mandy?"

She recognized the throaty voice. "Yes, hello, Mrs. Ponsonby." She rolled her eyes at her mom and dad.

"Say we're busy!" Dr. Adam whispered, almost tottering from his stool at the sound of the name.

"Listen, my dear, I know your mother and dear Adam must be terribly busy . . ."

"Yes, actually they are." Mandy pulled another face. "It's not Toby, is it?"

"Toby? Oh, no, dear, he's quite recovered, thank you. No, what I was wondering was could you possibly pass on a message? It's about foxes."

Mandy grew more interested. "Have you seen some

at Bleakfell Hall?" She wondered if the pair from Upper Welford had made their way down into the valley after all.

"Not seen, exactly. But I have definite evidence that there are foxes in my garden. I got back home this evening to find that my garbage pails had been ransacked. The lids were off and there were cans and waste paper strewn all over the yard. Absolutely no doubt in my mind that foxes were responsible. And that makes me rather worried about my poor Pandora and Toby. I mean to say, foxes are such vicious creatures. What would happen if brave little Toby were to try and chase them? He could be terribly injured."

"Oh, I don't think a fox would —" Mandy got no further with her sentence.

"I've been speaking to Sam Western about the problem, and he agrees with me. We feel we should record all our sightings and find out their preferred spots. Then, when we've established a pattern of their movements, it will be much easier to track them down and drive them out."

Mandy clenched her teeth and kept silent. She knew there was no point in arguing with Mrs. Ponsonby once she got a bee in her bonnet.

"I volunteered to organize things. I call it our Fox

Watch program. We need to find out how many foxes there are prowling around our yards at night, and to warn people to keep their pets indoors, just in case. I promised to tell everyone in the village, so that we could set up an early-warning chain of phone calls whenever anyone sights one of these pests. And that's the message I'd like you to pass on to your parents, Mandy, dear. If anyone at Animal Ark happens across any sign of a fox, please telephone me and let me know immediately!"

Mandy stuttered out a promise. "Fox Watch!" she cried as soon as she put down the phone. "Mrs. Ponsonby can't know for sure that it was foxes who upset her pails. She wasn't even there!"

Grandma listened and calmed her down. "Now you know what Mrs. Ponsonby is like. She is prone to exaggerate. I'm sure other people in Welford will take a more sensible view of the foxes. 'Live and let live' is the motto."

"Yes, and anyway, it's nearly Christmas," Grandpa added. "The spirit of goodwill should reach Mrs. Ponsonby eventually. In other words, she'll probably get over this fox business sooner than you think. I wouldn't worry about it if I were you."

So Mandy let herself think that it was a storm in a

teacup. She listened to the grown-ups planning a carol-singing group to go around and visit all the houses in the neighborhood the following night.

"If we can't have our usual Christmas Eve carol concert outside the Fox and Goose because of this big TV star ceremony, we'll just have to fix up an alternative," Grandma said. "We'll wrap up warm in our hats and scarves and go around singing all the old favorites."

> "*Good King Wenceslas looked out,*
> *On the Feast of Stee-phen!*"

Dr. Adam piped up.

"We'll collect money for a children's hospital charity. Would you and James like to come?" Grandma asked.

> "*When the snow lay round about,*
> *Deep and crisp and ee-ven!*"

"You bet!" Mandy was back in a good mood. Now it really *was* almost Christmas!

*   *   *

> "*Christmas is coming,*
> *The goose is getting fat . . .*"

Dr. Adam strode up the drive to Upper Welford Hall. He rang the doorbell.

*"Please put a penny
In the old man's hat!"*

Sam Western opened the door. He frowned at the band of carol singers, led by Dr. Adam. Behind him was a group of a dozen or more, hats pulled well down, song sheets fluttering in the stiff breeze. Mandy and her grandparents were among them, though her mom had had to stay on call at Animal Ark. Mrs. Ponsonby had insisted on coming. And there was James and another friend, Susan Collins, as well as Ernie Bell and his old pal, Walter Pickard. The two old men growled and grunted their way through the songs, stamping their feet and looking forward to a nice warm fire and a drink back at the Fox and Goose.

Dr. Adam rattled the collection box. "All for a good cause," he said cheerfully.

The landowner dug into his pants pocket, then demanded another song for his money. The singers struck up "The Twelve Days of Christmas." Mandy could hear Mrs. Ponsonby belting out the words at the top of her voice.

"Thank you, thank you, and a Happy Christmas!" Sam Western cried, when they reached the fifth day.

> *"On the fifth day of Christ-mas*
> *My true love sent to me . . .*
> *Five go-old rings!"*

"Whoa, thank you. I'll catch my death of cold out here!" Briskly he stepped back and closed the door.

Then there was much scuffling and nudging as the band turned and went down the drive, flashlights raking across the perfect lawns, feet crunching on the frosty gravel. At the gate, Grandma took charge and headed them all off to High Cross.

"Lydia will give us a better welcome than we got here," she promised. "So come on, raise your voices one more time!"

Mandy and James hung back as the others went ahead to Lydia Fawcett's old-fashioned farm. Their throats were dry, their fingers tingling with cold.

"That's where the foxes headed off to, remember?" James said quietly. He pointed toward the stone cross on the hill, known locally as the Beacon. It was a land-mark for miles around.

Mandy shone her flashlight up the hill, listening to the

new song. "We shouldn't stay too long," she warned. "They'll think we got lost."

James took no notice. "Maybe the foxes are still around." He left the path and stepped onto the rough heather. "If we're lucky, we might see them."

"If they are, I'm definitely not letting Mrs. Ponsonby know!" Mandy was still worked up about last night's phone call. She told James about the Fox Watch scheme, and the cruel plan to drive the foxes out of the village.

"Shh, hang on!" James caught her arm. "Switch your light off, Mandy. Look up there: It's them!"

Instinct made her crouch low among the frozen heather beside James. She looked up the slope, toward a clump of hawthorn trees, feeling the silence gather. There on the brow of the hill, she saw the foxes.

They were dark shadows in the moonlight. But as Mandy's eyes grew used to the dark, she could pick out more detail. "You're right, it's the same ones!"

"Shh!"

"What are they doing?" The foxes were rolling on the ground near the trees, then jumping up and chasing their own tails.

"Playing," James whispered.

"At this time of night?" Mandy crept closer and spot-

ted a movement in one of the trees. "Look, James, there's an owl up there on that low branch!"

The big, pale bird sat staring at the foxes, chest feathers puffed out, eyes unblinking.

As the foxes whirled in tight circles, still chasing their tails, they steered nearer and nearer to the hypnotized owl.

"He'd better watch out!" Mandy whispered. The foxes were almost within reach of the bird. They pretended to ignore the owl, but Mandy could see what they were up to. Once they were close enough, the foxes would stop playing and pounce.

Around and around they went, somersaulting and bucking, as if they'd taken leave of their senses. The unwary owl was fascinated.

Then, as they raced around the tree trunk, directly underneath the owl, one fox leaped up at the branch with snapping jaws.

Crack! Mandy and James heard the sharp teeth snap shut. The owl flapped its wings and rose from the branch just in time. The fox fell back to the ground, disappointed.

"Phew." James breathed again. "I've never seen anything like that before!"

"Amazing." Mandy backed off as the foxes sniffed around the trunk then ran off, still hungry.

"They were trying to fool the owl into thinking they hadn't seen him!" James watched the two doglike animals melt into the shadows of the trees.

Now that the foxes had gone, Mandy wanted to hurry and join the others. They jogged down the path to High Cross Farm and arrived just in time to sing the last song for Lydia. Miss Fawcett stood at her door, arms folded, smiling and humming along. At the end of the song, she invited the whole crowd inside for a drink.

"What were you two up to out there?" she asked James as she gave him a mug of cocoa. "I noticed you creeping up when it was nearly over. You didn't nip into the barn to say hello to my goats by any chance?"

"No. We were up by the Beacon. We saw two foxes!" he told her.

"But don't tell anyone!" Mandy broke in. "Mrs. Ponsonby thinks they should be driven out."

"Ah, yes, I heard." Lydia Fawcett smiled gently. "Fox Watch, isn't it? Don't worry, I won't let on."

"Thanks." Mandy knew the secret was safe with Lydia. Though she was a farmer, she held unusual views about wild animals like rabbits and foxes, refusing to let others shoot them on her property. "These foxes were doing something strange. They tried to fool an owl into thinking they hadn't seen him, and they managed to get close enough to grab him."

"Almost," James nodded. "But not quite."

Lydia smiled again. "Sly old things. Were they running rings around him?"

Mandy nodded. "Chasing their own tails. It was like they hypnotized the owl."

"That's exactly what they did. Foxes are well known for it." Lydia confirmed what James and Mandy had just seen. "They're very clever animals. It's what people mean when they say foxes can charm the birds out of the trees!"

The carol singers left High Cross Farm and trooped down the hill into the village, calling at houses on the way. The collection box was heavy and jangling with coins, and their voices were hoarse, as at last they turned down by the side of the church for a final call at the Old Vicarage.

"'While Shepherds Watched'!" Mandy's grandma suggested, with a stern eye on Mandy and James. "And no fooling around with the words this time!"

The singers gathered at the bottom of the steps and struck up the first verse.

"While shepherds washed their socks by night,"

Mandy sang.

"All seated on the ground . . ."

"Mandy!" Dr. Adam warned out of the corner of his mouth.

She grinned up at him. But just on the burst of the next line of the carol, she saw her mom's car pull up in the drive. She turned and ran to meet her.

"Hi, Mandy. How did you all do?"

"Fantastic. We saw the foxes trying to charm an owl!"

Dr. Emily put an arm around her shoulder and walked toward the door. "I meant the carol singing."

"Great. But what are you doing here?"

"Oh, I was on my way home from another call and I just thought I would pop in and take a second look at the Dixons' pups before they send them all off to nice new homes."

"Can I come, please?" Mandy never missed a chance to help her mom and dad. She saw the door open in answer to the carol singers, and Mrs. Dixon appeared with a handful of loose change.

"Sure. Stand to one side while the thirsty hordes head for the Fox and Goose." Dr. Emily waited for the carol singers to disperse. "Mandy's coming with me. We won't be long," she told Dr. Adam. They arranged to meet up with him and Grandma and Grandpa Hope at Lilac Cottage. James had already been met by his own dad, and soon there was no one except Mandy and her mom left in the driveway.

"Come on," Helena Dixon said. She had her fingers hitched through the collar of a fully grown collie, who wagged her tail furiously and gazed at her with intelligent eyes.

"This must be Henrietta." Dr. Emily stopped to pat the dog as she went in.

The gorgeous Henrietta! Mandy smiled to herself. The dog certainly was beautiful. Her dark eyes were big and wide, her sharp ears were pricked above her fine, long face. And she was an all-over bundle of energy and fun, just like her pups.

"You said on the phone that you wanted to check the puppies," Mrs. Dixon said with a frown, leading them through to the back of the house. "I take it there's nothing wrong?"

"Well, I'm not certain, so I thought I'd better come back and see. I've been reading up about a condition which is quite common in this breed." Mandy's mom sounded businesslike.

Suddenly alert, Mandy followed. The pups were being kept in the utility room, as before. They barked and bounced with joy when the light went on, and they saw their visitors.

"I do hope there isn't a problem," Mrs. Dixon said

with a sigh. "We've already found homes for three of the pups. I wouldn't want anything to go wrong now."

"Well, let's see." Dr. Emily decided to begin with Henrietta herself. She took a strong light from her pocket and shone it directly into the dog's eyes.

Mandy watched. Why did her mom want to examine the mother as well?

"There's an inherited weakness in collies," she explained. "It's called collie eye, but to be more exact, it's CEA, or collie eye anomaly." Next she picked up one of the puppies and shone the light into his eyes.

"Meaning what?" This was bad news as far as Mrs. Dixon was concerned. They heard irritation in her voice.

"It's a disease of the retina inside the eye. The retina can become detached, and then of course the dog will go blind. There's some level of CEA present in a high percentage of collies, unfortunately." Dr. Emily moved on through the second and third puppies, examining their eyes under the strong beam of the flashlight.

"Here's Flora." Mrs. Dixon handed her the fourth puppy.

"Fine," Mandy's mom said. "Now, Nipper, let's take a look at you." She took the last pup from Mandy. He squirmed and wriggled, trying to lick their hands.

When she stood up she was frowning.

"Well?" Helena Dixon wanted the verdict.

"First, I'm pretty sure Henrietta does have some level of CEA. As far as I can tell from a quick examination, she only has partial sight in her left eye. Now, it's not severe enough to be a big problem for her, thank goodness, and of course she can make up for sight loss through her hearing and sense of smell." Dr. Emily gave a full, calm explanation.

"What about the puppies?" Mandy realized that Henrietta might have passed the condition on to them. She felt her stomach curl into a tight knot as she held on to Nipper and stroked his soft head.

"Flora, Daisy, Olivia, and Henry are clear." Dr. Emily slipped both hands into her pockets and studied the fifth puppy. "But it was Nipper I was concerned about. He didn't seem to have a good sense of direction when we first saw him, and you remember he kept tripping over things?"

Mandy nodded. Her hands began to tremble.

"That's what made me come back. And I'm afraid I was right about him. Nipper does have quite a high level of CEA in both eyes."

"You mean he's blind?" Mrs. Dixon tried to grasp the full picture.

Mandy hugged him to her.

"No, not completely. But his vision is very restricted. The problem is, collie eye can lead to the retina becoming completely detached in future years. And then of course, the dog would become blind."

Nipper's pink tongue rasped along Mandy's knuckles as he begged for her to stroke him again.

"And what do you suggest we do?"

The four healthy puppies skidded along the tiles, playing and yelping, while Henrietta sidled up alongside Mandy and Nipper.

"Of course, the decision is up to you. Some owners are prepared to keep a dog with poor eyesight. It takes a lot of extra patience and care, but it can be very rewarding. All these dogs are extremely friendly and loyal, and you would find the same thing even in one with a disability. On the other hand, breeders are keen to screen out the gene responsible for CEA, so they might suggest putting the puppy down."

There was a horrible pause. Mandy swallowed hard and waited for Mrs. Dixon to reply. Her hand shook as she stroked Nipper's head.

"Would it be difficult for us to find an owner for him?"

"Possibly. But he's an affectionate little pup. Maybe someone will be willing to take him."

"Oh, I don't know. No one has chosen him so far; perhaps because he's obviously so much of a handful. And now we know why," Mrs. Dixon sighed. "Perhaps it would be kinder . . ."

She didn't speak the words, but Mandy knew full well what she meant. *Perhaps it would be kinder to have Nipper put to sleep!*

"Take your time. Don't decide right away," Dr. Emily suggested.

"Yes, you're right. I'll talk to my husband." Helena Dixon began to show them out. She took Nipper from Mandy and carried him with her through the house to the front door. "Can we give you a ring when . . . if . . . you know . . . ?"

"Of course." Dr. Emily said she was sorry about the news. "I wish I could have given them all a clean bill of health," she sighed. "But do call me at Animal Ark as soon as you've talked it through."

Mandy hardly knew what she was doing as she got into the car and they drove off. She was breathing shallowly and her whole body was tense.

But she knew she couldn't say anything. After all, her mom was just doing her job like a good vet should. They had no right to interfere with the Dixons' decision.

As they drove past the church, the moon lit up the

clock face on the square tower and the golden weather vane glinted. It swung around in the wind.

Will they? Won't they? Would Helena Dixon decide that half blind, Nipper was too much of a nuisance after all? And would she have him quietly and gently put to sleep?

Four

With the death threat hanging over Nipper, the days before Christmas for Mandy grew bumpier still.

"Mrs. Ponsonby!" Jean sounded a warning note as a car pulled up in the clinic parking lot early the next day. Dr. Adam and Dr. Emily disappeared swiftly into the treatment rooms.

"Ah, Mandy, my dear!" The Terror of Welford strode in with a dog tucked under each arm.

Mandy hadn't reacted quickly enough to get out of her way.

"No, no, don't disturb your mother and father. I know

47

what busy people they are! You and Jean will do just as well." She deposited Pandora, her overweight Pekingese, and Toby on the floor and delved into her oversized handbag for a batch of yellow leaflets. "Now, listen, the clinic is an ideal location to hand out our Fox Watch warning pamphlets. Here they are, hot off the press. I need you to give out one of these to every single person who comes in. Is that clear?"

Jean took the pile and Mandy glimpsed the contents over the receptionist's shoulder. "BEWARE FOXES!" she read. "Keep Your Eyes Peeled for Welford's New Menace, the Urban Fox! Report any sightings to Fox Watch Program Leader, Mrs. A. Ponsonby."

Jean took off her glasses and shook her head. "Is this really necessary? I mean, I always consider it rather a privilege myself whenever a fox ventures into my little garden."

She spoke meekly, but Mandy could have hugged her for sticking up for the much-insulted fox.

"Hmph!" Mrs. Ponsonby could see that Jean needed advice. "My dear, it's people like you who make Fox Watch's task so much more difficult. You entice them into the village with your ill-judged saucers of milk and leftovers from the dinner table. And where does that leave us? We're overrun with the creatures before you can turn around!"

"But I haven't seen a fox in a long, long time." Jean protested her innocence.

"Then you should come to Bleakfell Hall and see the damage they do in my yard."

As Mrs. Ponsonby spoke, Toby and Pandora scuttled behind the desk and riffled through Jean's wastebasket. Mandy bent down to pet them so that Mrs. Ponsonby didn't see her face turn red with irritation.

"This morning I went out and what did I find? Two garbage pails turned upside down and all their contents tossed out! Chicken bones and bacon rind devoured. Orange peel chewed by sharp teeth. Quite disgraceful!"

Jean sighed. "I'll have to ask Adam and Emily if it would be all right for you to leave your leaflets here." She disappeared into a treatment room, leaving the door open.

"Tell them that Mr. Western is standing by with a group of fellow farmers. As soon as we've acquired a sufficient number of sightings in the village, their intention is to pin down the foxes' homes and flush them out!"

Mandy stood up with a sharp intake of breath. "But, Mrs. Ponsonby, you know what that means, don't you? The farmers around here hate foxes. They won't just drive them out of the village, they'll shoot them as well!"

"Nonsense, dear. It will be quite sufficient for Sam Western to use his knowledge of the creatures to chase them out of the neighborhood. He can block up the entrances to their dens, do whatever's necessary. But he doesn't actually have to destroy them. Don't be so silly."

Mandy opened her mouth to protest again, but her dad emerged before she could frame a sentence.

"Good morning, Mrs. Ponsonby."

Mrs. Ponsonby gave him a dazzling smile. "Good morning, Adam. Please call me Amelia!"

"Um — er — Amelia, I'm afraid we can't take these leaflets from you. We have a policy here at Animal Ark never to take advertisements from outside bodies, and that would apply to Fox Watch, I'm afraid." He pushed the pile back across the desk, polite but firm.

Mandy wanted to cheer.

Mrs. Ponsonby's face fell. "But this is hardly an advertisement, Adam. After all, we're not trying to sell a product."

"No, but Emily and I feel we have to hold very strictly to our rule," he insisted. "I'm sorry."

Try as she might, Mrs. Ponsonby couldn't get him to change his mind. In the end, she had to put the leaflets back inside her bag and go off to try at the post office and the village hall for spaces on the bulletin boards to announce her program.

"Well done, Dad," Mandy sighed. She watched Toby and Pandora jump into the back of Mrs. Ponsonby's car and drive off. "But I wish Mr. Western and his men weren't on her side." She pictured them getting together, driving the foxes into the corners, raising their guns, and shooting.

Dr. Adam winked. "Don't worry, love. Your average fox can outsmart Sam Western and Amelia Ponsonby any day!"

*   *   *

The clinic that morning was full of two topics only: Mrs. Ponsonby's Fox Watch and the forthcoming appearance in Welford of the famous Joe Wortley.

". . . A friend of the Dixons," people said in awed tones.

". . . Staying with them over Christmas."

". . . My sister, Wendy, saw him in a Range Rover with Helena Dixon!"

". . . So handsome, just like he is on TV!"

Mandy came and went, filling in at reception for Jean when she popped out on her lunch break. When the phone rang, she had trouble hearing what the speaker said because of the excited gossip about Friday night's grand celebration.

"Hello, this is Animal Ark clinic. Who's this, please?"

"This is Helena Dixon. May I leave a message for Emily Hope, please?"

It was the phone call Mandy had been dreading. She steeled herself to hear the Dixons' decision about Nipper. *Yes, go ahead.* With one hand over her ear to cut out the noise in the waiting room, she held her breath.

"It's about the puppy with the eye disorder. We talked it through last night and decided that the best thing to do was to have him put down."

Mandy felt her heart thud and miss a beat.

"Are you still there? It seemed for the best. I wanted to call you earlier this morning and arrange for it to be done as quickly as possible. But now I'm afraid it's been taken out of our hands."

"What do you mean?" Mandy gathered her wits after the shock.

"Well, we knew that Sophie wasn't happy with the thought of it. In fact, she was rather upset. She went to bed in a very strange mood. This morning when she got up, she asked if she could take Henrietta and the two remaining puppies for a walk. That was Nipper and Olivia. The other three had been taken off to their new homes before breakfast."

It was hard to concentrate on Mrs. Dixon's voice. Mandy thought of all the dreadful things that might have happened during the walk.

"Well, Sophie had her way and took the three dogs out. I knew something was wrong when first Henrietta and then Olivia came back to the vicarage alone."

"Why, what's happened to Sophie and Nipper?"

"That's the point. I was frantic, about to call the police. Sophie had been gone for hours. I'd even been out to look for her myself. Then, when she did turn up at last, she was in a dreadful state. Her shoes were covered in mud and straw, and her new jacket was torn. She said that Nipper had run off and got lost, which is just like him, of course. The poor girl had hunted everywhere, but in the end she just had to come home without him."

"You mean, Nipper is still lost?" Mandy gripped the phone, trying to piece together the full picture.

"Exactly. Goodness knows where he went. But at least it does solve one problem."

"What do you mean?"

"Since he's got himself lost, we don't have to ask you to put him to sleep for us. In fact, it's an impossibility. I thought it best to let you know."

"He could freeze to death!" Mandy had cycled to the Hunters' house as soon as she could. "Poor little thing — the temperature drops way below freezing at night. James, what are we going to do?"

"We should go out and look for him." James settled his glasses firmly onto his nose and considered the problem. "If it was any other lost animal, that's exactly what we'd do right now."

"But the problem is, if we do find Nipper and take him back to the vicarage, the Dixons will only bring him to Animal Ark to be put down!" Mandy couldn't bear to think about it. "They will, James. I'm absolutely sure!"

"But if we don't find him, he'll either starve or freeze." James faced facts. "Which would you rather have?"

"Neither!" She paced up and down the Hunters' kitchen. "He's out there somewhere, probably scared and in danger. We don't even know how well he can see with this eye disease. He could wander over the edge of a cliff up in the field, or fall in the freezing river — anything!"

"We can't just leave him, can we?" James waited for Mandy to agree.

"No." It was hard; one of the worst decisions she'd ever had to make. But when it came to it, it was better to have Nipper put to sleep by someone who cared.

"Let's go," she whispered. "Come on, before we change our minds."

They rode out on their bikes and searched high and low for the lost puppy. They called in on the farms, from Graystones in the valley to High Cross on the hill, at the small terraced cottages in the main street, and the grand houses set back from the road. Everywhere the answer was the same.

"No, sorry, Mandy love, there's been no collie pup around here. But we'll call Animal Ark if we do spot him." Walter Pickard leaned on his garden gate and promised to help if he could.

"Poor little thing!" Marjorie and Joan Spry came to the door at The Riddings and cried out in unison. Their wrinkled, birdlike faces were full of concern. "No, we certainly haven't seen him here, have we, Marjorie?"

"Unfortunately not, Joan. But we will look very hard and telephone you if we find him!"

Mandy and James thanked the elderly twins and went on from house to house.

The only person who didn't seem to care about Nipper was Mrs. Ponsonby at Bleakfell Hall.

She was on her way out when they cycled up the drive. "Tut-tut!" She shook her head. "Trust the Dixons to lose a dog. Such a careless sort of family: That was my impression right from the start!" She locked her front door and waved good-bye to Toby and Pandora, who yapped through the window at her. "Poor dears, they don't like being left in the house alone. But it would be dangerous to take them with me today!" she said darkly, raising her eyebrow in a sinister way.

"What do you mean?" Mandy let James scoot off to look around the big garden while she stayed with Mrs. Ponsonby.

"Fox Watch!" The old lady mouthed the words. "Shh! I don't want to worry Pandora!"

Alarmed, Mandy glanced around. "Have you seen a fox?"

"No, not here. But I've just had a phone call from

Dennis Saville up at the Hall to say that the foxes have been spotted. Mr. Western has ordered him to round up the men to go and flush them out. Of course, as leader of the Fox Watch scheme, it's my duty to go and supervise arrangements! We're meeting in a quarter of an hour." She was in a hurry to be on her way.

Mandy's thoughts flew from Nipper to the foxes. She felt certain it was the same pair as the ones she and James had seen twice before. "Where are they?" She bent down to peer through Mrs. Ponsonby's car window.

"Somewhere up near the Beacon. Now, dear, you must let me go. They need me to organize things. I should get up there in double-quick time!"

As Mrs. Ponsonby drove off, James trotted back and picked up his bike. "No sign," he reported. Then he caught sight of Mandy's worried face. "What's wrong?"

She gasped and gabbled out the news. "They're going to shoot the foxes!" Surely by now Mrs. Ponsonby must realize that was what Mr. Western intended. She stared aghast at the disappearing car.

"Oh, no, they're not!" James said with fierce determination. He didn't even stop to think. "Come on, Mandy. If we get up there before they do, we can scare the foxes away!"

She leaped into action after him. Soon they were pedaling furiously out of the village, up Moor Lane toward the Beacon. They ignored a wave from Walter Pickard outside the pub, and didn't even stop to talk to Dr. Adam, who was driving back from a call at one of the farms on the moor.

"Where's the fire?" He stopped the car and leaned out, but Mandy and James sped by.

"Can't stop now!" Mandy yelled. They pedaled on. Breathless, their legs aching from the effort, they followed Mrs. Ponsonby. Her car wound up the road ahead of them and there, by the ancient stone cross, was a bunch of men, already gathered to take care of the foxes.

"See, they *have* got guns!" Mandy said, using her last ounce of energy. Five dark figures stood around, hands in pockets, long shotguns resting in the crooks of their arms. She could make out Major, Sam Western's big German shepherd, sniffing around at the base of the cross.

"Let's hope we're not too late!" Head down, James kept pedaling. "We need to try and find out exactly where the foxes were last spotted. Then we can go and make as much noise as possible."

"The men won't like it. They'll try and stop us," Mandy warned. She wasn't scared of them and their guns, but she knew it wouldn't be easy. "Look, they've spotted us!"

They saw Dennis Saville break away from the group and come toward them. He waved his arms and shouted at them to go away. Then there was another yell, and the men moved off quickly toward the brow of the hill, following Major as he picked up a scent. Mr. Saville doubled back after them.

"Too late," Mandy whispered. The dog had definitely found a trail. He bounded out of sight on the far side of the hill. The gang of hunters broke into a run, then strung themselves out in a line on the horizon. They put their guns to their shoulders and aimed into the next valley.

But James refused to give in. "Not yet, it isn't!" He ditched his bike and began to run across the field.

Mandy knew there was nothing to do but to follow. She, too, flung down her bike and cut across the rough, heather-covered ground.

By this time Mrs. Ponsonby did seem to have realized exactly what was going on. She got out of her car and began to protest. "Mr. Western, what on earth is happening? Why do you need those guns? My Fox Watch program is only meant to drive the foxes out of Welford. I didn't intend for you to come out and shoot them!"

The men ignored her. Her wailing voice was lost in the wind.

There was a sharp crack, then another and another. Puffs of smoke rose in the air as the guns went off. *Bang! Bang! Bang!* Mandy felt her heart jolt and shudder.

James came to a halt, his face suddenly white. He turned and stared at Mandy.

Mrs. Ponsonby stood frozen to the spot. The dog barked, the men shouldered their guns, then dipped out of sight.

With stiff, leaden legs, James and Mandy forced themselves to follow, dreading what they would find when they crested the hill. The gunshots had cracked through the air and dashed their hopes.

"You were right." James reached the top and stared down. "We were too late."

Mandy saw an animal lying quite still. It was almost too weak to move. Only the pure white tip of its bushy tail twitched feebly.

The men had scattered over the hillside, kicking at low bushes and peering under boulders where a fox might hide. They'd left their first quarry to bleed to death and were busy hunting down the second.

Mandy ran to the shot animal and crouched over it. It was the dog fox, wounded in the side, but still alive. His sides heaved, and a dark trickle of blood stained the ground.

Quickly she unwrapped her scarf from her neck and held it against the wound. "We've got to stop the bleeding!" she insisted, as James came up beside her. "If we can just do that, then maybe he stands a chance!"

The fox lay on his side, amber eyes staring up at her.

They were too shocked to notice another figure following them over the freezing ridge. The man ran toward them quickly, but it wasn't until he joined them

by the injured fox that Mandy looked up and recognized her father. Behind him, she saw the stout figure of Mrs. Ponsonby laboring up the hill.

"Let's have a look," Dr. Adam said quietly. He saw in a moment what had happened. He took the bloody scarf from Mandy and held it firmly in place, but he shook his head as he studied the fox. "It's bad," he warned. "I don't think there's much we can do."

Mandy bit back the tears. "Try, Dad!"

He took off his jacket and covered the animal to keep it warm, but he knew from its condition that it was no good. "I'm afraid he's bleeding internally as well."

Helpless, they had to stand by and watch the fox die.

After what seemed like forever, the shuddering breaths stopped and the heaving sides were still.

Dr. Adam leaned forward, closed the fox's eyes, then stood up. "What about the vixen? Did she escape?"

"I think so." James was the one who answered. He blinked hard and turned away from the body.

They stood staring down at the half dozen men who had killed the fox. The hunters searched on for the vixen, but Major had lost the scent and was zigzagging aimlessly across the hill.

"They don't care! They left him to suffer and die!" Mandy cried. Tears streamed down her cheeks. She choked and couldn't say any more.

Dr. Adam took up the dead fox and went to meet Mrs. Ponsonby before the men returned. Mandy felt herself being helped gently into the Animal Ark Land Rover, but she was in a daze. She hardly knew where she was or who was there, only that a dreadful thing had happened.

Nothing could make her feel better, not her dad's kind words, nor Mrs. Ponsonby's heartfelt apologies, nor her mom's comforting arms when they arrived at Animal Ark late in the afternoon.

Mandy told her what had happened.

They were hard facts, dragged out from the depths of her own suffering: "Oh, Mom, one fox has been shot dead, and the other is being hunted up in the field. And to make things worse, poor Nipper is lost in the freezing cold!"

Five

"Mom says the vixen is probably safe," Mandy told her grandfather the next morning. He'd called to persuade her to come out of the house and help him put the finishing touches on the lights in the village square. It was Thursday, and Joe Wortley was due to switch them on at seven-thirty the next evening.

"We can't have you moping around the house when there's so much to do," he'd insisted.

"I don't feel much like it, Grandpa." Mandy had hardly slept. She felt washed out and unhappy, unable to get the picture of the dead fox out of her mind.

"Come on, the fresh air will do you good. I've had

strict orders from your grandma not to let you get away with saying no!"

So, to please her grandparents, she'd wrapped up in her jacket, scarf, and hat and come to help. The tall Christmas tree stood outside the door of the Fox and Goose, opposite the church. It rose almost as high as the roof of the pub, with colored lights strung through its branches.

"Well then, at least one of the foxes lives to fight another day," her grandpa said now, standing back to judge the effect of the lights in the tree. "Adam tells me he knew something was badly wrong the moment he saw you and James hurtling up the hill on your bikes. He decided he'd better follow and see what was up."

"I'm glad he did." She sighed. "If Dad hadn't come, I'd always have wondered if there was anything we could have done to save the fox." Her lip quivered as she remembered the wounded fox's amber eyes staring up at her.

Just then, a Range Rover cruised down the main street into the pub parking lot. Mandy saw Joe Wortley and Sophie Dixon get out. The television star went into the Fox and Goose, leaving Sophie to cross the road and head for home by herself. When she saw Mandy, she ducked her head and rushed on.

"Watch out!" Mandy yelled, as another car sped by.

Sophie had been so busy ignoring her that she hadn't seen it. The driver braked hard and skidded as Sophie stepped back. An accident had been narrowly avoided.

"Are you okay?" Mandy ran across.

"Fine, thanks." The girl's pale face had turned bright red. "I just wasn't looking where I was going."

An alarmed driver glared out of his window at her before he straightened his car and drove off. Mandy's grandpa watched from a distance to see that everything was all right.

"Have you found Nipper yet?" The question popped out before Mandy had time to think. Since Sophie had been doing her best to avoid her, it was obvious that she didn't want to talk about the lost puppy.

She shook her head and the curtain of black, shiny hair swung across her face. "I've looked everywhere."

"I'm sorry about his eyesight," Mandy said quietly.

This time Sophie nodded once. "Thanks." She bit her lip. "Would this disease hurt? I mean, would he be in pain with it?"

Mandy answered as best she could. "I don't think so. It just makes his vision go blurred. Why?"

"Nothing. I was wondering, that's all." Sophie changed the subject. "We found a home for Olivia this morning. That's the last of the puppies. She went with her new owners after breakfast." She put on a cheerful smile. "Well, I'd better go now."

"No, listen!" Mandy walked with her across the road. "About Nipper; have your parents really made up their minds about him?" She still clung to a shred of hope that the puppy might be found.

"Mommy has. She says it would be much too much trouble to look after a handicapped dog. She called someone who breeds collies at the place where we bought Henrietta. The man there said that pups with collie eye should definitely not be allowed to breed."

"But that's not the same as having him put to sleep!" Mandy insisted. "Anyway, Henrietta is the one who passed it on to Nipper. According to this man, he should never have sold Henrietta to you in the first place!"

"Try telling Mommy that." Sophie shrugged and walked on down the path. "Anyway, it's beside the point now. Nipper ran away and that's all there is to it."

"It was below freezing last night." Mandy had checked the thermometer, as usual. "If he was out in the open, you realize what could have happened to him?"

Sophie twirled around. "I know! You don't need to tell me!"

"Sorry." Mandy stepped back.

"Look, he ran away, okay? I let him off the leash to

play, and the next thing I knew he'd vanished! I looked everywhere for him but I couldn't find him!" Sophie glared angrily at Mandy.

"Where were you when it happened?" In her own mind, she began to plan another search. She would call for James. Together they would try again.

"Out of the village somewhere, by a big house. Oh, I don't know!"

"Which house? Was it up in the field or down by the river?" Mandy put her hand on Sophie's arm.

"Like I said, just outside of the village. I don't know the name of it, do I? I've only just moved here!" She turned away to shake Mandy off.

"Sorry, I didn't mean to upset you," she murmured. Sophie obviously cared about Nipper, but she seemed edgy and secretive.

"Look, leave me alone, will you! It's bad enough without having to answer all these questions." Her gray eyes flashed out a warning. "The way you're all going on about it, anyone would think I'd lost Nipper on purpose!"

Sophie's bad temper only made Mandy more determined to carry on with the search. She went back to help her grandfather put the finishing touches on the tree, but all the time she was making plans.

"What's going on inside that head of yours?" Grandpa Hope asked as they slid his stepladders into the back of his van, ready to drive back to Lilac Cottage.

"What do you mean?" She blushed and smiled.

"You're too quiet for my liking. It usually means you're up to something."

"Me?" Mandy didn't mind being teased. As she climbed into the passenger seat, she decided to tell him all about Nipper, knowing that he would understand.

"That's a hard one," he admitted. He cleared the steamed-up windshield and turned the ignition key. "I've never even heard of collie eye. They always look like such a fit and active type of dog." Before they set off for home, he turned to look at her. "Do I take it you're going to carry on with the search?"

She nodded. "I'll give James a call after lunch and see if he wants to come, too."

"No need. Here he comes now." Grandpa pointed to a figure speeding down the main street on a bike. "It looks like he's just come from your place and he's in a mighty big hurry."

James squealed to a halt beside the van. "Your mom said I'd find you here!" he gasped. "I was looking for you in case you wanted to come out and look for Nipper with me!"

Mandy grinned. "Great minds think alike."

"But listen, something else has come up." He hardly paused for breath. "It's Mrs. Ponsonby. I think she's gone fox-mad!"

"Oh, no, not again!" Mandy's heart sank. As if it wasn't enough that the bossy, interfering lady had already been partly to blame for one fox's death. "What's happened now?"

"She's just brought Pandora into the clinic with an injured paw. She's going on and on about a fox attacking the dog, demanding to see a vet, telling everyone it's an emergency."

Mandy drew a deep breath. "Not again! Did she actually *see* a fox attack Pandora this time?"

James shrugged. "I don't even know how bad the paw is. When I saw Pandora, her foot was wrapped up in a big towel. Jean took the dog straight into a treatment room, partly to stop Mrs. Ponsonby from making such a fuss. Mr. Saville was in the waiting room with Major. I noticed him listening to Mrs. Ponsonby to find out what was going on, then he got up and left. I came straight down here to let you know." He pushed his hair from his forehead and breathed at last.

"What do you want to do; go ahead and look for Nipper, or go back and sort out Mrs. Ponsonby first?" Grandpa could see that Mandy was torn between two missions.

"Animal Ark," she decided, thanking James and telling him to sling his bike into the back of the van and climb in. "It'll only take a few minutes to find out what's happening. I'm worried about Dennis Saville as well," she confessed. "We don't want Mr. Western and his men poking their noses in again."

So they chugged off in the van, arriving at the clinic just as Dr. Emily emerged from the treatment room to give Mrs. Ponsonby news of Pandora's injury.

"How is she?" Mrs. Ponsonby cried. "How is my poor precious darling?"

"She's going to be okay. It isn't a deep cut, so she doesn't even need stitches. I've cleaned it up and left Simon to wrap it up with a bandage." Dr. Emily stood with her hands in the pockets of her white coat. She glanced up at Mandy and gave her a smile as she came in.

"Not a deep cut?" Mrs. Ponsonby quizzed. "Are you sure? There was an awful lot of blood!"

"Not really. It looked worse than it was."

"But Pandora was attacked by a fox! And they have such sharp, vicious teeth."

Dr. Emily put her head to one side. "A fox?"

"Certainly. There's no doubt about it. I heard a dreadful clattering noise out in the yard, so I knew the greedy creatures had come back to raid my garbage. I got there just in time to rescue poor Pandora from serious injury!"

"Hmm. It doesn't look like the sort of injury a fox would inflict, Mrs. Ponsonby. The cut is too clean for a start. A fox would tear the flesh in a more jagged way. No, I'd say this was done by a sharp edge; something like the rim of a can, for instance."

Mrs. Ponsonby sniffed and shook her head. "No. It was the fox who got away from Mr. Western's men yesterday. I'm convinced of it. To tell you the truth, the fox scares me. Living alone in my big house isn't easy. Any sudden noise or unwelcome visitor is very alarming, especially at night. And, of course, poor Pandora and Toby are frightened of him, too."

"Her," Mandy said quietly.

Everyone turned to look.

"Pardon?" the fussy old lady said.

"Her. It's a vixen. The dog fox is dead."

"Well, whatever." Mrs. Ponsonby squared her shoulders and prepared for battle. "As soon as I can get Pandora safely tucked up in her basket at Bleakfell Hall, I'll be on the phone, organizing my Fox Watch group to drive the pest out once and for all!"

Six

"She means it, Mandy!" James tried to yell over his shoulder as they pedaled hard for Bleakfell Hall. "Mrs. Ponsonby is dead set on chasing the vixen out of the village!"

"Not if we have anything to do with it." Mandy gritted her teeth. "Anyway, it's not Mrs. Ponsonby I'm worried about. It's Mr. Saville and Mr. Western." The farm manager must have rushed back to Upper Welford Hall to tell his boss where the fox was now. It was vital for her and James to get to Bleakfell Hall before they did.

Given Dennis Saville's long drive up Moor Lane,

that shouldn't be too difficult, she decided. Once they reached the gateway to Mrs. Ponsonby's old house with its towers and tall chimneys, she slowed down. She gazed up at the crumbling stone walls and arched windows and noticed Toby barking madly from a downstairs room. "It's okay; we made it," she gasped, glancing back down the road for Mr. Western's car. "No one's here yet."

"Let's go around the back and take a look." James dismounted and pushed his bike past the stone steps leading to the old doorway. "Didn't Mrs. Ponsonby say that the fox comes to raid her garbage pails in the yard?"

Mandy nodded. The back of the Hall was even more run-down than the front. A door to an outhouse had come off its hinges and stood propped against the wall, and long icicles had formed on the leaking gutters. "This place gives me the creeps," she muttered.

"Look, those must be the stables." James pointed to a row of divided doors shut and bolted at top and bottom. They hid their bikes behind a wall and went cautiously across the yard. "I wonder when they last had any horses in them?"

"Centuries ago, by the look of it." Mandy shivered. The yard was covered in a thick frost, and in one corner she spotted the garbage pails. "See!" She pointed to a row of rusty, old-fashioned metal pails. Some of the lids were missing, and one was tipped onto its side.

"What a mess." James frowned. Scraps of paper blew here and there, a tin can rolled and knocked against a wall.

"Wait a minute!" Mandy had gone to take a closer look. As she bent to stand the pail upright, she noticed tracks in the frost. "James, look! Footprints!"

He ran across to study the light marks, the padded foot and sharp nails of the animal that had raided the pails. "What kind are they?"

Mandy looked twice, then three times. She had to be sure. The footprints were delicate. The creature was small and doglike. There were also marks where a long tail might have brushed the ground. "They're fox-prints," she whispered with a sinking heart.

"It looks like Mrs. Ponsonby was right, then." Here was the evidence in front of them. James sighed. "Now we can't keep on saying the fox is innocent."

"So what? She's only doing what comes naturally. Wouldn't you take advantage of what people threw away if you were a fox?" Mandy stuck up for animals against people as usual. "What harm does it do?"

"Hang on, I'm not arguing with you." James only half listened. "There's a spot of dried blood in this corner and another one by the pails! I wonder how they got there."

But then he picked up another set of tracks. "Mandy, come and look at these. They're different!"

She followed him toward the stable doors. The new tracks were more scuffed. This time the shape of each footprint was human. The prints led straight to the peeling door of the stable farthest from the house. "Whoever it is, they're still in there!" Mandy breathed. The tracks stopped at the door and didn't come out.

"How did they get in there in the first place?" James tried the door. The bottom half was bolted from the outside.

"Through here?" She took hold of the top half of the door and felt it swing open with a loud creak. "Watch your head, James!"

He ducked just in time. "What now?"

"Listen, did you hear something?" Mandy peered into the dark, musty stable. Her voice echoed in the empty space. "A kind of whine. There it is again!" She braced her arms against the bottom section of the stable door and got ready to vault over.

"It sounds scared," James whispered.

"It's not the only one!" As her eyes grew used to the dark, Mandy made out a heap of old straw in one corner of the stable. There was a rusty manger and old bridles hanging from hooks on the wall. Above her head, a loft ran the length of the rough, disused building. As she looked up, a dusty cobweb brushed her face and made her jump.

"Hang on, I'm coming in after you." James jumped over the door and followed. "Mandy, are you thinking what I'm thinking?"

The whining grew louder. It was definitely coming from the pile of straw. "That it might not be the fox?" Small furry footprints, a whining noise turning to a yelp as they crept toward the corner. "Nipper?" she said softly.

The straw rustled and shifted, then a tall figure stood up out of the untidy heap. Sophie Dixon glared at them. She held a squirming puppy in her arms. "What do you want now, Mandy Hope?" she demanded in an angry, scornful voice. "Why can't you mind your own business just for once?"

"We want to help," James said, once he got over his surprise and Mandy had introduced him to Sophie and Nipper. "You don't need to worry, we're on your side."

"You won't tell anybody I lied?" Sophie set the puppy down in his straw bed.

"No. But how did you find this place?" James wanted to know the full story.

"I didn't. Nipper did. He did run away when we were out on our walk; that part was true. But I didn't lose him, I followed him here. I think he could smell the leftovers in the garbage pails, so he sneaked in through the back gate. I was going to yell at him and take him home, then it just came to me in a flash: why not hide him here? No one would know. I could come secretly every day and look after him. It would have worked, too, if you two hadn't barged in."

"I can see why you did it," Mandy said slowly. For the first time she saw that Sophie Dixon was nicer than she seemed. Anyone who went out of their way to help an animal was okay in her book. "But what did you think you could do in the long run? I mean, you can't keep Nipper locked away in Mrs. Ponsonby's stable forever."

"Why not?" said Sophie, still resenting their interference.

"Well, for a start, he needs fresh air and exercise."

"I can come and take him for walks without being seen, can't I?"

"But he needs special care because of his eyesight. And he needs company. He's going to be lonely in here all by himself."

Sophie sighed. She had no answer to this. "Okay, if you're so clever, what would you have done?" She glared at Mandy.

It was Mandy's turn to shake her head and sigh. Suddenly, a lot of things fell into place: the reason why Henrietta and Olivia had arrived back at the vicarage before Sophie, the fact that Sophie's shoes had been covered in mud and straw. And hadn't Mrs. Dixon said that her daughter had been upset by the news about Nipper? But still, finding her here with him now came as a complete surprise. Mandy went to stroke the puppy, giving herself time to decide what they should do next.

"I did it to save Nipper's life!" Sophie pleaded. "If you give us away now, they'll do what they were going to do in the first place!"

"It's okay, I've already said we won't tell." James stepped in again. "Will we, Mandy?"

She felt the puppy's rough tongue lick her hand. "What if he needs treatment?" she said quietly. She didn't know enough about collie eye to be sure that it was safe to leave it untreated.

"You told me yourself he wouldn't be in any pain!" Sophie flashed back at her, taking Nipper into her own arms.

"Yes, but I can't tell if it'll get any worse. We know that he can still see a bit, it's true, but Mom would be able to tell us more if we asked her."

"No!" came the quick, fierce answer.

"Okay, not yet at any rate." James stepped in between

them. "Listen, you two, I think I just heard a car coming up the drive!" He put his hands up and warned them not to go on arguing.

"You're right!" Mandy listened to the crunch of car tires over gravel. "But it doesn't sound like Mrs. Ponsonby." The noise of the engine was deep; more like a Land Rover than the little car used by the owner of Bleakfell Hall.

"Mr. Western?" James craned his head over the stable door to investigate. "It's no good. I can't see!"

"You'd better hide Nipper," Mandy urged Sophie. As she helped to cover them both with straw, she explained why they suspected the landowner and his manager might have come in search of the fox.

"Shh! I can hear voices!" James pulled the door closed. Now they were in total darkness. The straw rustled, Nipper whimpered, while Sophie calmed him. "Try to keep him quiet," James warned.

Mandy went to join him. "What can you hear now?"

"Men. At least two of them. Listen, you can hear them talking."

Car doors slammed, footsteps came around the side of the house. There was the faint sound of Toby barking from inside the house. Then Mandy heard them speak, too.

". . . Not back from the vets' yet."

"It makes no difference. If she says the fox was here, she'd want us to take a look."

Now Mandy knew that James had been right. It was Dennis Saville and Sam Western. Their heavy feet tramped into the stone-flagged yard.

The muffled voices of the two men grew louder. She heard Dennis Saville give a short laugh. "After yesterday, I'm not so sure. She didn't sound too happy when she saw us with the guns."

"Well, what did she expect? I suppose she thinks you

can track down a fox and ask him politely if he'd mind leaving the premises!" Mr. Western was scornful as he poked among the pails. "There's been a fox here all right."

Mandy held her breath. *Please let Nipper keep quiet!* Now the footsteps approached the stables.

"And something else by the look of it." Dennis Saville's gruff voice was right outside the door. "These prints here are more like a dog's. Hey, wait a minute!"

James and Mandy prayed hard.

"These are human footprints, too!" Saville had spotted the new set of prints made when Mandy and James had investigated the stable.

It would only be seconds before the two men tried the door, moments until they were discovered. Now all they could hope was that they could bluff their way through without giving Sophie away. They gritted their teeth and prepared themselves.

Just then, another car drove up and stopped. It made the two men hesitate.

"It sounds like the Fox Watch lady herself," Sam Western muttered. "She'll have seen our car. I suppose we'd better go and tell her where we are and what we're doing here."

But before they could get halfway across the yard, Mandy heard Pandora's excited yap. She pictured the little Pekingese hurtling around the side of the house, bandaged leg or not. "Down!" Mr. Western said roughly, as Pandora barked and growled.

Then Mrs. Ponsonby came into the yard, hot on the heels of her angry pet. "Mr. Western, Mr. Saville, put those guns down!"

James allowed himself a big sigh of relief as Mrs. Ponsonby's loud voice echoed off the walls. Mandy could just see his face in the gloom. "Phew!" she whispered. Behind them, Sophie and Nipper shifted position under the straw.

"We heard the fox was back," Sam Western began.

"But did you hear me ask for your help?" Mrs. Ponsonby demanded.

Pandora yapped and snarled, and now they could hear Toby's rougher bark as a back door was unlocked and the mongrel came bounding out of the house.

"No, but Dennis here heard about your problem at the vets' this morning. Naturally we thought . . ."

"Well, you thought wrong, Mr. Western. I'm not a violent woman, and I certainly don't believe in guns. If I'd thought that you intended to employ them, I would never have included you in my Fox Watch program."

"Good for her!" James whispered. His eyes glinted and he smiled at Mandy.

"We're farmers, Mrs. Ponsonby. What did you expect?"

"Knowledge and expertise, Mr. Western. Not brute force!" Obviously Mrs. Ponsonby could stand her ground. "Down, Toby! Down, Pandora! Now, you will please do as I request and put away your guns."

"What about the fox?" Dennis Saville made one last appeal.

Mandy pictured Mrs. Ponsonby drawing herself up to full height in her bright red winter coat and hat. There was a long pause before she gave her reply. "As leader of the Welford Fox Watch program, rest assured, Mr. Saville, you can leave this fox to me!"

Seven

"That was close!" James waited until they heard the sound of the landowner's car making its way back up Mrs. Ponsonby's drive. Then he went to tell Sophie it was safe to come out.

She emerged with her hair in a mess and bits of straw sticking out of her polo-neck sweater. "Why is everyone going on about this fox? What's so special about it?"

Mandy explained that the vixen's partner had been killed by the farmers the day before. "We don't want the same thing to happen to this one. In fact, we'd do anything to save her!" As she spoke, she watched Sophie's face closely. Once more she got the feeling that the girl knew more than she was saying. Her gray eyes had the same guarded look as they'd had when she'd lied about the lost puppy. She turned her head sideways and pretended to be interested in something in the far corner of the stable.

"What would you do to save her?" she challenged when Mandy had finished.

"Anything!" Mandy repeated. "Why?" She saw from James's frown that he was as puzzled as she was.

"Hang on a minute!" Sophie went to the door and opened it a fraction of an inch. "All clear," she whispered. "Mrs. Ponsonby has taken those noisy dogs of hers into the house. It doesn't look as if she's going to come snooping around in here, thank heavens." She drew a slim silver flashlight from her pocket and turned it on.

For some reason, Sophie Dixon had begun to annoy Mandy once more. Perhaps it was her secretive expression. To Mandy's surprise, she found herself sticking up for Mrs. Ponsonby. "I'd have thought she had the right to snoop around inside her own stables!" she retorted, ignoring James's astonished look. "And Toby and Pandora aren't any noisier than other dogs would be if they saw strange men in their yard!"

"Okay, okay, keep your hat on." Sophie shone the flashlight toward the rickety wooden loft above their heads. "I don't know why you're defending her. Isn't she the one who wants to get rid of your precious fox?"

"At least she doesn't want her killed!" Mandy felt herself go hot. If it hadn't been for the fact that she didn't want to dash off without solving the Nipper problem, she wouldn't have stayed in the stable a moment longer.

"Look, do you want to save this fox, or not?"

"Of course we do."

"You're not acting as if you do."

"Why, what do you know about her?"

"More than you think."

"Ha!" Mandy turned away, exasperated. What was the point of trying to carry on a conversation with someone as difficult as Sophie Dixon?

James's frown deepened. "Why are you shining the light up there?" The yellow beam swung across the roof and down onto an ancient ladder that led from ground level to the loft.

Sophie turned it on his face. James's glasses glinted in the light, as he put his hand up to shield his eyes. "If Mandy would just stop arguing, I could show you something."

"What?" Mandy demanded.

"Shh! You'll have to be quiet." She clicked off the flashlight and slid it back in her pocket. "Otherwise she might not come out."

Plunged into sudden darkness again, they stood and waited. Mandy felt the puppy come sniffing around her ankles, but she hardly noticed. "Who might not come out?" she whispered urgently.

"Guess." Sophie spun it out as long as she could.

"The fox," James supplied the answer in a low whisper. "You've seen her up there in the loft, haven't you?"

"Twice. Last night and earlier this morning. She's still up there now, only you two have probably frightened her into hiding."

For a few moments there was silence. Was it true? Or was Sophie having a cruel joke at their expense? The more she thought about it, the more Mandy could see how the vixen might have fled down from the field after the shock of seeing her partner killed. Maybe she would hole up in a dark, deserted place like this. After all, she knew she would be safe from the farmers, and she could keep warm and dry. And then there were the prints in the frost by the garbage pails, and Mrs. Ponsonby's claim that a fox had attacked Pandora.

"Don't you believe me?" Sophie whispered. "Well, come and see."

She led the way up the ladder, knowing that they would follow. James went next, putting one foot on the rickety bottom rung. "Are you coming, Mandy?" he whispered.

Mandy nodded and followed. The ladder creaked. She heard Sophie reach the top and step into the loft. If the fox was up there, she would certainly know she was being cornered. She might be frightened and perhaps try a sudden, wild dash for freedom. Yet the only way down was by the ladder. Mandy climbed as quickly as she could, anxious to get it over with.

"Wait here." Sophie ordered them to stay by the ladder. "We don't want her to escape."

They crouched under the rafters, able to make out an old stack of hay bales in one corner. "Is that what she uses as her den?" James asked.

Sophie nodded. "You should see her climb up here. She moves like lightning."

He turned to Mandy. "I can smell her, can you?"

Taking a deep breath, Mandy's nostrils filled with a sharp, unmistakable stink. She knew then that Sophie had been telling the truth.

Then she heard a rustle of straw, and saw the tip of a pair of pointed black ears. There were bright orange eyes staring at them through the darkness, a long snout, a flash of white chest as the fox eased its head from behind one of the bales.

"Come on, let's go down!" James had seen enough. "We're scaring her."

Fumbling, half-slipping, they made their way down

the ladder. Nipper greeted them by dashing and barging straight into their legs, tangling himself up in feet and straw. Sophie picked him up and dusted him off.

"What do you say now?" There was a small grin on her face as she confronted James and Mandy.

"I'd say she chose a pretty good place to lie down and rest," James said. "Except that now we know she's here."

"Yes, but none of us is going to give her away!" Mandy said. Then she stopped short. "Are we?" She looked from James to Sophie, her eyes widening into a stare. "Oh, no!" There had to be a reason for Sophie showing them the fox's hiding place, and at that moment Mandy knew exactly what it was.

Sophie stared her down. "That's right. You said you'd do anything to save the fox. Well, I won't give her away if you promise not to tell a single soul about Nipper!"

It was blackmail, but James and Mandy had to agree.

"I feel dreadful. Nipper shouldn't be locked up in that dark stable," Mandy said as they cycled back into the village.

"No, but I suppose I can see why she's doing it," James answered quietly. "She's trying to save his life."

Mandy thought about it. "He's safe for today, and so is the fox, as long as we don't say anything. But what about tomorrow? What's going to happen in the long run?"

"I don't think Sophie knows yet. But from the way she's behaving, I'd say she was pretty desperate. She can only take it one day at a time."

As they reached the village square, Mandy stopped and sighed. "This is what you'd call a stalemate, isn't it?"

James nodded. "At least the fox is safe," he repeated.

"If Sophie keeps her word."

"She will." He sounded sure of this much.

So they bicycled off on their different ways home. By the time Mandy reached Animal Ark and passed her mom on her way out of the clinic, she was still feeling confused.

"How do the Christmas lights look?" Dr. Emily asked.

"What? Oh, fine, thanks." Mandy went straight into the house to find her dad cooking soup for lunch.

He handed her a steaming bowl and a hunk of crusty bread. "Eat this, it'll warm you up."

"Oh, okay, thanks, Dad." Mandy sat and picked up her spoon, then paused with it midway to her mouth. "Dad, is it cruel to keep a blind dog alive?"

"It depends on the circumstances. Why do you ask?"

"No special reason." She reddened and put down her spoon without eating. "But when would it be cruel?"

"Only when the condition causing the blindness is painful for the dog. Dogs have excellent hearing and sense of smell, as you know. That makes up for their loss of eyesight. You can still take a blind dog for walks. He'll probably want to stay pretty close to you, and you have to be patient and understanding. You have to speak to the dog more often than usual, so he can get his bearings, and so that he's not too lonely."

"Hmm." Mandy narrowed her eyes and stared out of the window at the frosty scene.

Dr. Adam studied her face. "Come on, love, what's up?"

"Nothing, Dad, honestly."

"Yes, there is. I can tell. Has it got anything to do with the collie pup — what's his name? Zippy, Nippy . . . Nipper, that's it!"

Mandy ducked her head and pretended to blow on her hot soup.

"I thought he was missing. The Dixons didn't seem to have tried too hard to find him, poor little pup." Again he looked closely at her. "Mandy?"

"I can't say anything, Dad. I promised." Now she kicked herself for bringing the subject up in the first place.

Dr. Adam sat down opposite her. He waited a while before he spoke again. "Listen, Mandy, I don't know exactly what the problem is here. But it looks like you've got yourself into a situation you'd rather not be in. Is that right?"

Tears gathered as she looked up and nodded. Her dad was being kind again. "Stop it, or I'll cry," she warned.

Dr. Adam dipped into his pocket and handed her a big hankie. "Blow your nose on that. That should cure it." He wrinkled his nose and grinned. "Better? Oh, dear, I feel a piece of good advice coming on. Do you mind?"

She dabbed and sniffed. "No. Go ahead."

"Well, then. Don't take on too much responsibility. If this has got something to do with rescuing another animal in trouble and you find that for once you can't solve the problem by yourself, or even with James's level-headed help, then maybe it's best just to take a step back and let someone else help to sort it out instead." He spoke gently, without prying or trying to boss her. "After all, it is nearly Christmas!"

"That makes it worse." *Poor little Nipper, alone in the cold stable.*

"And you're sure there's nothing we can do?"

"Thanks, Dad, but no." Mandy stood up without touching her soup. "Do you mind if I don't eat it? My tummy feels all knotted up."

"It sounds like a hard promise you made back there!"

"It is," she sighed. "Very hard. As a matter of fact, two lives depend on it!"

Eight

"Hello, Mrs. Dixon. Is Sophie in, please?" Mandy stood at the door of the Old Vicarage. In the background she could see Henrietta plodding from room to room, looking as if she'd lost something.

"Hello. It's Mandy, isn't it?" Helena Dixon looked harassed. "As a matter of fact, she isn't. She was here for lunch, but then she slipped out again. She's behaving very oddly at the moment."

"How come?" Mandy was disappointed. It had taken a lot of nerve to face coming here to talk to Sophie again. A dozen times she'd changed her mind; yes, it would do some good, then no, it wouldn't, then yes, it would.

"Well, this morning, for instance, I asked if she wanted to come to Walton to go Christmas shopping with me, and she said no. That's not at all like Sophie; she loves shopping. Then after lunch I wanted her to take Henrietta out for a walk, but when I went to look for her in the TV room, she wasn't there. Now I've no idea where she is."

I bet I do, Mandy thought. But she said nothing.

"Poor Henrietta's been moping since the last pup left for her new home. I thought a walk would do her good." She looked hard at Mandy. "I don't suppose you would take her for me? Of course, I'd pay whatever you normally charge."

"I'll do it for nothing," Mandy said promptly.

"Are you sure? Wouldn't you like some extra pocket money for last-minute Christmas presents?" Mrs. Dixon had already lifted the dog leash off its hook by the door. Henrietta came bounding across the hallway in a flurry of white, black, and brown fur.

"No, thanks. How long do you want me to keep her?"

"Well, I've promised to pop back to Walton to meet Joe and Andrew, my husband. Would it be all right if you brought Henrietta back in a couple of hours?"

They made the arrangements, then Mandy and Henrietta set off, up by the church and down the main street. The dog wasn't especially big, but she was strong, Mandy found. She pulled at the leash, dodging into doorways and sniffing at corners. "Hey, who's taking who for a walk?" she cried, when Henrietta spotted Ernie Bell's cat, Twinkie, and shot across the road after him. She barked and tugged, almost pulling Mandy off her feet.

Twinkie waited until the last moment, then zoomed off, up the path to his home at the end of a short row of terraced houses.

Ernie's grizzled head appeared around his front door. "Can't you keep that dog under control?" he yelled. "Oh, Mandy, it's you. I hope you're taking that wayward dog in hand and giving it a few lessons on how to behave. It's been a real menace to Twinkie ever since it came to live in the vicarage."

Mandy gathered her breath as Henrietta jumped up at the gate and rattled it with her front paws. "Sorry, Ernie. I'm supposed to be taking her for a walk, but it's turning out to be the other way around!" It was true; Henrietta certainly needed some proper training. "It's not her fault, though. She's a lovely dog, deep down!"

"And I'm Santa Claus," the old man grumbled, disappearing indoors again.

"Take no notice, young miss," Walter Pickard

chipped in. Walter lived four doors down from Ernie. "You know what he's like; always grabbing the chance to have a good moan. Especially at Christmastime." He winked at Mandy and grinned at the unruly dog. "Mind you, you have got your hands full there."

Henrietta wanted to be off. She was straining at the leash, almost pulling Mandy's arm out of its socket.

"She doesn't get enough exercise," Mandy gasped. She staggered down the street, slipping and sliding on the frosty pavement. "See you soon, Walter!"

"Tomorrow night!" he promised. "That's when they have this big do to switch on the lights, isn't it?"

"Will Ernie be there, too?" It seemed as if the whole village was coming.

"You bet he will. As soon as he heard they were handing out free refreshments, he made up his mind to be first in line. When did you ever hear of Ernie turning down something for nothing?"

"Now, just hang on a minute . . ."

Mandy heard Ernie's door reopen and the old grumbler's gruff voice start up again. She would let them sort it out between them, she decided. Anyway, Henrietta was well on her way to McFarlanes' post office, and she couldn't have stopped her if she'd wanted to.

"Hi, James, hi, Blackie!" Mandy waved at them as they came out of the shop.

"Whoa!" James yelled. "Where are you off to?"

"I don't know. It doesn't look as if it's up to me!" Henrietta charged on.

"Can we come anyway?" James and Blackie quickly caught up. James glanced at Mandy's hot face and windswept hair. "Did you volunteer to do this?" he asked.

"Kind of." Mandy began to think that Henrietta had picked up a trail. "I stopped at her house to talk to Sophie again."

"About Nipper?"

"Yes. I wanted to try and persuade her to take him back home." In spite of her dad's advice, Mandy still felt she had to do something. The idea of leaving the puppy in Mrs. Ponsonby's dark stable gnawed away at her. "I thought that if I talked to her again, she might listen to reason!"

For a few moments James said nothing. "But she wasn't there?" he asked.

"No. I think I can guess where she is, though."

"It looks like Henrietta knows, too." James saw how the dog pulled at her leash, nose to the ground. They were heading out of the village now, toward Bleakfell Hall. "Mandy, do you think we ought to risk it? What if Sophie's there when we arrive? She'll think we've broken our promise."

Mandy was determined. "Why should she? We could be going to check that the fox is still okay, for all she knows."

"But we're not, are we?"

"Yes, in a way." Mandy couldn't separate the fox from the puppy. She felt somehow that their fates were linked.

"James, I've talked to Dad, and he says even a blind puppy can be trained to live a good life. You don't have to put them down just because they can't see. And Nipper isn't even completely blind! But if we try to tell the Dixons that, Sophie will say we've broken our promise, and she'll tell Mrs. Ponsonby about our fox. I've gone over and over it, and in the end I decided that the only thing we could do was get Sophie to persuade her mom and dad to let her take Nipper home after all."

"Just like that?" James said doubtfully. He kept Blackie on the leash as they came within sight of the big gates leading to Bleakfell Hall.

Mandy pulled hard on Henrietta's leash and managed to make her stop. They stayed hidden behind the high garden wall. "Have you got a better idea?" she asked.

"Well, I suppose we can't leave Nipper in the stable much longer," James admitted. "I've been thinking about the poor little thing ever since we left him there with Sophie this morning."

"Me, too. Dad says blind dogs need even more company than normal dogs, otherwise they get lonely and miserable." It was getting harder to hang on to Henrietta as they talked it through. The dog snuffled at the gatepost, nosing here and there in the grass and flower borders.

James stood on tiptoe and peered over the wall. "Mrs. Ponsonby's car's in the drive," he reported. "And the lights are on in the house. That means she's at home."

"Yes, and Sophie's probably in the stable with Nipper right now as well," Mandy reminded him. She didn't think she had the strength to hold Henrietta back much longer. "I'm going down the side of the yard to take a proper look. Are you coming?"

James followed, careful not to let Blackie make any noise. They had to crouch and creep forward, out of sight of the downstairs windows of the Hall, in case Toby and Pandora were on guard. Their feet crunched over frozen leaves in the ditch. Low branches that hung over the wall snared them and caught in their hair.

"Henrietta can hardly wait to see Nipper again," Mandy whispered, as she felt the dog pull and strain. "I'm sure she's picked up the scent, James!"

He nodded. "See that double gate?" They turned a corner around the back of the house and its grounds and looked along the length of another stretch of wall. "That must lead into the yard. We might be able to get in there without being seen."

Mandy guessed that it was the entrance Sophie had been using, too.

"It's okay, we can stand up straight now," James said. The wall was tall enough for them to run freely toward the gate without being seen.

"Only one more minute!" Mandy promised the impatient Henrietta. Then they would be in the yard and safely across into the disused stable.

Her heart raced, her arms ached as she glanced at James, and the two dogs came to a sudden halt outside the gate.

"What is it, Blackie?" James whispered. The dog cocked one ear and whined. "What did you hear?"

"Henrietta heard it, too," Mandy said. They froze to the spot and waited. "Listen, there's someone in the yard!"

"Or *something*." James strained to pick up where the noise was coming from. "That sounds like a garbage pail being tipped open."

Mandy heard the scrape of metal, and then a sudden clang as the lid clattered to the ground. She stared at the peeling paint of the tall double gate, as if she might suddenly develop X-ray vision and stare right through it. There, in the bare, frosty yard, the phantom raider of Mrs. Ponsonby's garbage pails was hard at work.

A pail tipped and rolled with a hollow thud. They could hear wastepaper being kicked aside, and the lighter rattle of empty cans.

"It's the fox. She must be hungry," James hissed. His breath blew clouds of steam into the cold air. He put a hand on Blackie's neck to quiet him.

Henrietta looked up at Mandy from under her long fringe of white, black, and brown fur. She gave a high whine. "Shh!" Mandy dropped to her knees on the frost-covered grass to talk to the dog. "We know you want to see Nipper, but just wait until the fox has finished her dinner."

Henrietta's whine deepened to a growl. She couldn't understand why they'd stopped. Lifting one paw she scratched at the gate.

Mandy grimaced and gritted her teeth. "Shh!"

The collie studied the worn wooden barrier between them and her puppy and shook her tousled head. *"Yap!"* She gave a loud, sharp bark.

With their nerves already on edge, Mandy and James jumped out of their skins. Henrietta strained at her leash and scrabbled at the gate. Blackie joined in the fun. Now there was no chance that the fox would be allowed to go on eating in peace. "We'd better take a look," James sighed.

So they stood on tiptoe to peer over the tall gate, expecting to see a flash of a bushy red tail, a white tip, as the fox stole back into the safety of the stable. "Can you see anything?" Mandy whispered.

James shook his head. "Here, I'll give you a leg up, Mandy." He knelt and cupped his hands, waiting for her to step onto the support and clutch the top of the gate.

To do this, Mandy had to let go of Henrietta's leash. "Stay!" she hissed, without much hope that the dog would obey. Soon though, she was clinging to the gate and peering into the yard.

She gasped. "I don't believe it!"

"What?" James's arms sagged and gave way under her weight. He left her hanging from the top of the gate.

Then Mandy's own arms weakened. She dropped to the ground. "James, you're not going to believe this either!"

"What?" His eyes were wide and insistent. Blackie was still scrabbling at the gate, and Henrietta had begun to bounce up at it, too. Its old hinges creaked, the latch rattled.

As if in answer to his question, while Mandy still caught her breath and shook her head in disbelief, the rusty latch gave way. The gates swung open.

And now both Mandy and James could see clearly across the yard to the ramshackle area where Mrs. Ponsonby kept her row of old metal garbage pails. Instead of catching a glimpse of the bushy-tailed fox slinking off to her hideaway in the stable, they saw the real villain, nose still buried in the litter of paper, peels, and cans. Her tail wasn't long, her face not pointed, but flat, with a tiny snub nose. Her short legs waded through the wastepaper and one front paw was neatly bandaged.

"Pandora!" James's eyes almost shot out of his head.

The little Pekingese dog was concentrating so hard on gobbling the contents of the garbage pails that she didn't even notice her new audience. She snuffled, teased at a gnawed chicken bone, then tossed it in the air. Then she burrowed her head into the upturned pail and waggled her feathery tail as she discovered the next treasure.

Mandy and James stood in shocked surprise, while Blackie and Henrietta ventured through the gate. For a second, everything was quiet, then chaos broke out.

"*Woof!*" Toby bounded out of the house into the yard.

"Blackie, stay!" James gasped.

The black Labrador charged at Toby and greeted him as a long lost friend.

"*Woof, woof!*" Toby ducked and wove. He bounded toward Henrietta.

The collie leaped into action. Like a giant doormat, she flung herself at Toby. They met in midair and rolled to the ground, a mass of fur, legs, and tails. Blackie whirled around them, barking with all his might.

"It's okay, they're only playing," Mandy said. Toby was delirious with joy to find new playmates in his yard. Meanwhile Pandora guzzled her way through a half-eaten pork chop.

But the noise brought Mrs. Ponsonby rushing to the door. She was dressed in a tweed skirt and lilac sweater, long strings of pearls swinging across her chest. On her feet she wore furry purple slippers.

The owner of Bleakfell Hall seized a broom that stood by the door. She wielded it like a knight holding his spear and charging into battle. "Shoo, you horrid dogs!" she cried, her face red, her eyes glittering behind her gold-rimmed reading glasses. "Leave my poor Toby alone. Go on, shoo!"

Mandy glanced at the upturned pail. Pandora had moved on from the pork chop to a greasy margarine tub, oblivious of the chaos going on in the yard. And now Mandy's own eyes gleamed. *This is my chance!* she thought.

"Hang on," James warned, seeing what she was about to do. "Let's just think about this first!"

But Mandy knew it was their golden opportunity to

prove Mrs. Ponsonby wrong about the fox. She stepped forward and laid her hand on the arm that wielded the broom. "Er, Mrs. Ponsonby, would you just calm down a minute, please?"

"Shoo!" the old lady cried in a voice like a foghorn. She shook Mandy off.

"Would you please look at Pandora?" Mandy came back at her as Mrs. Ponsonby bore down on the trio of playful dogs.

"Not now, dear. Can't you see I'm busy?"

"But I think you'd like to know what she's up to," Mandy insisted, intent on getting their fox off the hook. All that was visible was Pandora's tubby little backside and feathery tail. The rest of her had disappeared deep inside the upturned pail. "It's not the fox who's been raiding your garbage. It's Pandora!"

Mrs. Ponsonby stopped in midstride. Her broom arm quivered, her jaw dropped. Then she swiveled around, following the direction of Mandy's pointing finger.

"What nonsense!" she began, refusing to believe the evidence of her own eyes.

"But it's true!" Mandy ran across to ease Pandora away from her grubby feast. Instead, the Pekingese squirmed farther into the pail and out of sight.

Mrs. Ponsonby shook her head. "You're making it up. And look, these dogs of yours are completely out of control!" Once more she began to jab with her broom at Blackie and Henrietta.

Mandy was down on her hands and knees, struggling to extricate Pandora, James was tugging at Blackie, and Mrs. Ponsonby was still parrying, when suddenly Henrietta broke away. The collie seemed to remember why they'd come here in the first place. She raced across the yard to the stables, running excitedly up and down, then pausing outside the stable where Nipper was hiding. She yelped and barked, sniffed at the door, then barked again. From inside the stable they heard a high, excited reply.

"*Yap-yap. Yap-yap!*"

"What was that?" All of a sudden, Mrs. Ponsonby's eyes and ears were razor-sharp. "Inside the stable; did you hear it?"

Blushing bright red, James shook his head. Mandy crawled out of the garbage and got to her feet. "Pandora's the one who's been stealing food from the pails!" she said, desperate to draw Mrs. Ponsonby's attention away from the stable. But Henrietta was mad with joy at the sound of her pup's voice. She barked and waited for another reply. From inside the dark stable, Nipper barked back.

"You see, that's how she hurt her foot," Mandy jabbered, following Mrs. Ponsonby across the yard. "Pandora must have cut it on an open can. It's obvious, isn't it?"

But Mrs. Ponsonby could move quickly when she wanted to, and nothing Mandy could say would stop her. She was already at the stable door, lifting the latch . . . and opening it.

"Oh!" Mrs. Ponsonby stopped on the threshold. Mandy and James came up behind. They peered in together.

There was Sophie Dixon standing silently in the gloom. Her dark eyes flashed with anger as she stared out at Mandy, ignoring Mrs. Ponsonby's gasp of shocked surprise. In her arms she held an excited puppy who barked and yelped as the light flooded in and he sensed his own mother. Henrietta had come to rescue him at last!

Nine

"It's not what you think!" Mandy told Sophie. She knew it looked as if she'd broken her promise and told Mrs. Ponsonby about the intruders in her stable.

Sophie looked at her with disgust. "You lied to me!"

"We didn't. You have to believe me!" Mandy gave up trying to hold on to Henrietta. She let the dog off the leash and watched as Sophie put the pup on the floor. Henrietta licked and nudged him, checking him from head to foot. Their tails wagged and they gave little yelps of pleasure.

"It's true." James added his voice. "We only came to try and persuade you to take Nipper back home." He spread his hands in a helpless gesture. "But then it all went wrong."

"Save your breath." Sophie glowered at them. "I don't even want to hear." There were tears in her eyes as she stooped to stroke Henrietta and her puppy.

"Excuse me a moment." Mrs. Ponsonby found her voice at last. "This all seems very strange!" She looked from Sophie to the two collies, then at James and Mandy. "Apparently everyone knows what's going on here except me."

"No, Sophie's making a mistake," Mandy began, still desperately trying to explain. "She's got it all wrong."

But the angry girl flared up again. "It's not me, it's you. You broke your promise and now I'm going to break mine!" She scooped Nipper into her arms again and went up to a bewildered Mrs. Ponsonby. "Did you know you've got a fox living in this stable?" she demanded. "It's in the loft right now. I saw it go up with my own eyes!"

Mrs. Ponsonby gasped and took a step back. "A fox?" she echoed. "Actually here in my stable? Is this true?" She turned to Mandy with a look of horror.

Sophie's eyes glinted with spiteful triumph. "I can prove it to you if you like."

But before she had a chance to take out her flashlight and shine it toward the dark loft, Mrs. Ponsonby had decided to believe her and panic had set in. "Toby, Pandora, come here at once!" she cried. "Help me, Mandy. And James, get hold of Blackie. We have to get these dogs out of here before the fox decides to attack!"

"She's probably more scared of us than we are of her," Mandy objected. At that moment she hated Sophie Dixon. Amidst all the noise and confusion, she pictured the poor fox cowering in a corner, her safe hiding place stolen from her by Sophie's betrayal.

"Don't argue, dear. That's right, keep hold of Toby. I've got Pandora. Now, let's get them out into the yard." She bustled ahead, only pausing once she was out in the fresh air to turn and make sure that Mandy and James were following. "Is everyone safe? Where's the girl from the vicarage?"

With Toby squirming in her arms, Mandy glanced over her shoulder, expecting Sophie to be coming after them with Henrietta and Nipper. But there was no sign of her. Instead, the stable door swung open. There were fresh scuff marks in the frost, and messy footprints leading toward the gate.

"She must have slipped away with the dogs," James muttered. "A good thing, too." He was as angry and disappointed as Mandy.

"Never mind now. I'll telephone her parents later on. What we must do first and foremost is deal with this fox!" Mrs. Ponsonby had gotten over her panic and begun to assume command once more. "I simply can't have the vicious thing taking refuge in there on a permanent basis. Goodness knows what damage it will do!"

Mandy recognized the tone of voice. There wasn't the least point in trying to argue. *Wait!* she wanted to say. *Where will the fox go if you drive her out of here?* The stable was her shelter from the winter cold. Wasn't it bad enough that she'd had to watch Sam Western and his men shoot her partner? Wouldn't it be the most cruel thing to send her on her way, out into the frost, all alone?

But she hung her head and remained silent as Mrs. Ponsonby strode toward the house.

The large woman halted on the doorstep to glance at the capsized garbage pail and trail of rubbish. "It's too bad," she tutted. She turned to Mandy and James. "This may seem cruel, and I know it's going back on what I said yesterday about not needing guns, but that was before I knew that the fox had actually come to live in my backyard!"

"Oh, no, please!" Mandy cried. "You're not going to bring Mr. Western back!"

For a moment Mrs. Ponsonby hesitated. But then she shook herself and squared her shoulders. "I'm sorry,

Mandy," she said at last. "I'm not a violent person by nature, believe me. But you must see that I really have no alternative!"

As the stout figure of Mrs. Ponsonby disappeared through the door, Mandy and James sprang into action.

"We're not going to stand by and let this happen!" she declared. They'd saved the vixen from Mr. Western before, and they would do it again.

"Come on, we'd better be quick!" he agreed.

Telling Blackie to stay in the yard, they ran back to the stable.

Mandy was the first to reach the ancient ladder leading to the loft, and she began to clamber up it, explaining what she thought they should do. "If we can get the fox away from here before anyone comes, at least she'll still have a chance!

"Whereas if we just leave her, the Fox Watch group will come here, and Mr. Western with his gun as well." James, too, had spotted the ruthless note in Mrs. Ponsonby's voice. "Where is she, Mandy? Can you see her?" he dragged himself onto the high wooden platform after her.

"Not yet." She peered into the pitch blackness, just able to make out bundles of straw and old hay bales piled haphazardly in one corner. "You know, we've only got Sophie's word that she's still up here!"

James took a deep breath. "Yes, but I can smell her. That means she's been here recently, even if she's not here now."

"You reckon she'll come back in any case?"

He nodded. Then he dropped onto one knee and pushed some straw to one side. He picked up a small bone, picked clean of meat. "Look at this."

Mandy crouched to study the chicken bone. The fox must have scavenged it from the garbage. And it was true, the smell of the fox was still strong and bitter. She would almost have said it was a hot smell. "I think she is still here!"

They listened. But there wasn't much time. Soon Mrs. Ponsonby would have made her phone calls and would be rushing back to take charge.

"Let's try the far corner," Mandy said. She pointed to the untidy stack of bales. "If she's up here, that's the most likely place for her to be hiding."

"I'll prop the door open so she can run straight out." James saw that it had swung shut since they'd climbed up to the loft. He went back to the ladder and began to climb down.

So Mandy crept forward alone on her hands and

knees, under the low eaves of the stable roof. "I'm very sorry," she murmured. "I know it looks as if we're driving you away, but it's for your own good!" If the vixen was hiding nearby, she hoped that a gentle voice would calm her.

She heard a rustle in the straw, then a faint whimper. Instinctively Mandy froze, hunched close to the floor, one hand on the nearest bale. There was another movement, and then a glint in the darkest corner of the loft. A pair of amber eyes stared.

Mandy held her breath. Now she could make out the whole face of the fox. She saw that the vixen was smaller and her head narrower than the dog fox that had been killed. She, too, was crouched, head down, her pointed ears twitching, waiting for Mandy to make the next move.

In spite of the danger the fox was in, in spite of Mrs. Ponsonby's panic and Sophie Dixon's meanness, for a moment Mandy was spellbound. She forgot everything except for the quick, clever beauty of the animal; her sharp face bordered with white, her black nose, and those deep gold, catlike eyes.

"Is she there?" James called from below.

His voice triggered the fox into action. Her ears flicked and there was a swish from her long, bushy tail. Then she opened her long mouth and flattened her ears.

Her teeth were white and pointed; dangerous sharp spikes for holding on to her struggling prey.

But Mandy didn't back off. "Yes," she called back. "I'm going to try to drive her down the ladder. Can you make sure she gets out of the door before Mrs. Ponsonby shows up?"

"I'll do my best. But hurry up, I think I just heard her come back into the yard!"

So Mandy made a crude lunge at the fox, intending to scare her out of the corner and down the ladder. The sudden, clumsy movement worked, for the vixen darted forward. In one lithe bound she cleared Mandy's crouching figure.

"Watch out, here she comes!" she called, whirling around to follow the fox's progress.

"I see her!" James held the door wide open.

But the russet-brown shape raced along the length of the loft, away from the ladder.

Mandy's heart sank. "This way!" she pleaded. At this rate, they would be too late. Mrs. Ponsonby would trap her again, Mr. Western would turn up, and all would be lost.

It seemed as if the clever animal understood that she had to get out. But she would do it her own way. When she reached the far end, she stopped and took a quick look over the edge, as if measuring the distance to the floor below. *No ladder for me!* she seemed to say. She sat back on her haunches and launched herself into midair in a flurry of straw. In a split second she had landed safely, sprinted for the door, and vanished.

"Thank heavens!" Mandy stood up and brushed herself off. She joined James at the door as Mrs. Ponsonby caught site of the fleeing fox.

"Pandora, Toby! Heel!" she screeched.

James raised his eyebrows and shook his head. Mandy shrugged. The last thing on the poor fox's mind was stopping to fight with Mrs. Ponsonby's dogs. She sped across the yard, past the garbage pails, and around the side of the house; a lean streak of rusty red, with a white flash of tail.

"Oh, dear!" Mrs. Ponsonby was red and flustered. "I promised Sam Western that I would keep the fox locked inside the stable. He's already on his way down from Upper Welford Hall. Mandy, dear, what happened? How did it escape?"

"He was too fast for us," Mandy mumbled, glad that Mrs. Ponsonby had a thousand and one things on her mind.

". . . And I called the Dixons to tell them that their daughter had been secretly hiding a puppy in my stable, and they said they'd come straight over, even though I tried to tell them that Sophie had already made herself scarce . . ."

"Well, we'd best be on our way, too," Mandy suggested. She didn't fancy being at Bleakfell Hall when any of these people arrived.

But Mrs. Ponsonby caught her by the wrist. ". . . That's not all. Finally I telephoned Animal Ark with my suspicions that you and James were tangled up in this situation, so your father is on his way, too! He asked me to tell you to stay where you were until he got here."

Mandy groaned and sagged.

"Not that I understand anything about what's been going on." Plump Mrs. Ponsonby looked and sounded out of her depth. "Why would Sophie Dixon need to hide that sweet little puppy in my drafty old stable?"

"Because nobody wanted him and she's afraid that her parents would want to have him put down," Mandy confessed quietly.

"Not want him? Have him put to sleep?" The color drained from Mrs. Ponsonby's face. "Whatever for?"

"Because he can't see very well," James explained. "There's something wrong with his eyes."

"You mean he's nearsighted?"

He nodded. "Something like that. It's called collie eye."

Mrs. Ponsonby took time to consider this. She drew a deep breath and her chest swelled. "Well, I can't see so well myself, but I hope nobody is considering having *me* put down!" She began to tut. Pacing up and down the yard, she took in the news that Mandy and James had just given her. "I know that not everybody adores dogs as much as we do, Mandy dear, but I would never have thought that a little vision problem is any reason for putting a puppy to sleep! And now I've made a mess of things by phoning the Dixons, haven't I?"

Mandy forgave her the moment she saw how much Mrs. Ponsonby regretted what she'd done. She went to pace alongside her. "Can't we stop them somehow?"

"How? Oh, Mandy, and it's nearly Christmas, a time of joy and good cheer! We should all be looking forward to it. But how can we celebrate with this great shadow hanging over that poor puppy's head? Oh, dear!"

"Not to mention the poor fox," Mandy murmured. But Mrs. Ponsonby was far too caught up in her worries about Nipper to hear her.

"Here comes a car," James warned, going around the side of the house to look. "I think it's the Dixons!"

And sure enough, by the time Mandy and Mrs. Ponsonby had joined him, with Pandora, Toby, and Blackie running excitedly between their legs, the big Range Rover had crunched to a halt in the front drive.

The tall, stern figure of Andrew Dixon jumped out first, slamming the driver's door behind him. Then Helena Dixon stepped down, her face serious as she held open the passenger door.

"Sophie!" Mandy gasped, as the Dixons' daughter appeared. She was white and trembling, her dark hair falling across her face. Her jeans were torn on one knee, her shoes muddy. She left Henrietta in the back seat of the Range Rover, but in her arms she held the tiny, half-blind pup.

"What? . . . How? . . ." For once, Mrs. Ponsonby was lost for words.

"We found them in the village, just about to get on a bus to Walton," Mr. Dixon told her. "The bus driver didn't want to let Sophie on board with Henrietta and the puppy because they were so muddy."

"Chasing across fields and goodness knows what," Mrs. Dixon put in. As usual, she looked immaculate in her tailored jacket and trousers.

Andrew Dixon took up the story again. "We received your phone call, Mrs. Ponsonby, and headed straight here. We passed by the bus stop just at the right moment. It seems Sophie's got an awful lot of explaining to do." He spoke quietly, as if he was trying to make up his mind about what was going on.

"Yes, and I don't see how she's going to come up with

a good reason for what she's done." Helena Dixon couldn't hide her disapproval. "She told us the puppy was lost, but it seems she's been lying to us right from the start!"

"It wasn't Sophie's fault." Mandy tried to help. She felt James tug at her jacket and saw his look of surprise. "Well, it wasn't! She only brought Nipper here and hid him because she wanted to save his life!" Much as she hated Sophie for giving the whereabouts of their fox away, she still had to give credit where it was due.

Mr. Dixon frowned, while his wife took him to one side. She whispered a hasty explanation. "The puppy is half-blind. I told Sophie it would be better to have him put down."

"You might have informed me first," he said, folding his arms and glancing at Nipper.

"I did, Andrew. But you must have been too busy to listen. You left me to make the decision, as usual. And now I'm the one who plays the baddie, just because it happens not to be what Sophie wants."

"Hmm." He scratched his chin and stared at his daughter.

Mandy bit her lip. This was like waiting for a verdict in court. Would Mr. Dixon side with his wife or his daughter?

Then Mrs. Ponsonby stepped in. "Never mind all that

now. What's past is past. I have an idea!" She had to raise her voice above the sound of another car as it approached along her drive.

Out of the corner of her eye Mandy saw the Animal Ark Land Rover arrive. But instead of going to greet her dad, she stayed glued to the spot to hear Mrs. Ponsonby's announcement.

"Let *me* take the puppy!" She strode over to Sophie and seized Nipper from her. "He's adorable. It makes no difference to me what his eyesight is like. He could be completely blind for all I care! I still think he's the most beautiful little pup! Yes, I do!" She held him up in both hands and wiggled him gently back and forth.

Mandy gasped. A home for Nipper out of the blue, from the very last person she would have expected!

"But . . ." Helena Dixon drew back her head in astonishment.

Her husband kept his eyes on Sophie, whose shoulders slumped as she slowly turned away and wandered toward their car.

"No, I won't hear any objections!" Mrs. Ponsonby rattled on. "I insist on giving the puppy a home here at Bleakfell Hall. We can't hear of him being put to sleep, can we, Pandora? Can we, Toby?" She cooed and dandled the puppy in front of them to let them all make friends.

By this time Dr. Adam had joined the group. "It might not be quite that simple," he warned. "If a pup has collie eye, he can be much more difficult to train."

Mandy frowned. Right away she saw what he was getting at. Mrs. Ponsonby might not have enough patience or even common sense to look after a special puppy like Nipper. After all, neither of her dogs was particularly well behaved.

Mrs. Ponsonby gave him a beaming smile. "Nonsense, Adam. You're talking to a dog expert, you know!"

"Yes, but, Mrs. Ponsonby . . ." he tried again.

"*Amelia!*" she reminded him.

Mandy saw her dad blush to the roots of his hair. She followed the argument, turning her head from one to the other like a spectator at a tennis match. On the one hand, any home for the puppy was better than none. On the other, she trusted her dad's opinion, and it was obvious that he didn't think that Mrs. Ponsonby had come up with a very good answer to the problem.

". . . Amelia," he stammered, "have you considered how Pandora and Toby would adjust to living with a partially sighted dog? They're used to having your attention all to themselves, you know."

"What are you suggesting, Adam? That I spoil my dogs?" Mrs. Ponsonby's voice rose an octave.

"Not at all . . . er, Amelia! I just want to point out the pitfalls."

"Nonsense, nonsense!" She waved away his objections and turned back to the owners. "Now, Mr. and Mrs. Dixon, it's up to you. What do you say?"

Ten

"I'm not sure." Andrew Dixon looked to Dr. Adam. "You're the expert. What do you think?"

Mandy and James hardly dared to move. Nipper's life hung by a thread.

"Come now, Adam, you think it's the perfect answer, don't you?" Mrs. Ponsonby was so involved in the brilliance of her solution that she failed to notice yet another car swing through her gates.

"Well . . ." Mandy's dad was just beginning to see the implications of his advice. "Don't look at me like that!" he whispered at Mandy as Mrs. Ponsonby dandled the puppy and cooed into his furry brown-and-white face.

In the Dixons' Range Rover, Sophie sat huddled, staring blankly at the hills behind Bleakfell Hall.

"Like what?" Mandy tried to hide her fears. But she knew she was biting her lip hard and digging her fingernails into the palms of her hands.

"Like I'm handing down a death sentence," Dr. Adam murmured, glad that Mrs. Ponsonby's attention had been diverted by the arrival of Sam Western and Dennis Saville. "What do *you* think we should do?"

"Let Mrs. Ponsonby keep Nipper?" she sighed. Sometimes a decision was too difficult for her ever to be sure.

But then, crises piled on top of one another. Before Adam Hope had delivered a verdict on Nipper, Mandy saw the hard look set into the lines on Mr. Western's face as he jumped down from his car and slammed the door. She saw a shotgun under his arm, and the muscular brown-and-black shape of Major trotting at his heels. Behind the landowner and his dog came the farm manager, Dennis Saville. He, too, carried a gun.

"I hear you have an unwelcome guest in your stable," Mr. Western said to Mrs. Ponsonby. He had no time for pleasantries. "And I understand you don't want any more dilly-dallying. Well, I'm glad to hear it." His voice was gruff, and he ignored the Dixons, Dr. Adam, Mandy, and James. There was serious business to be done.

"Yes, it's true." Mrs. Ponsonby still clutched Nipper as she went to confer with Mr. Western. "It gave me a terrible shock when I heard. Apparently, not only has it been raiding my garbage, but it's chosen my hayloft as its winter lodgings!"

"Well, leave it to us this time. Dennis and I will deal with it." He gestured for his manager to follow him across the yard.

Mandy and James stood between the two men and the stables. For a moment, Mandy set her mind against stepping out of the way. She glared into their faces, aware of the dull gray metal of their guns, the curved triggers and long thin barrels. But she knew they were wasting their time if they thought they could stride into the stables and make their kill. All they would find would be musty straw, an empty loft, and the sharp smell that the fox had left behind.

So she stood to one side, and felt James step in the other direction. Western and Saville pushed through the middle, ignoring Mrs. Ponsonby's hurried explanation until they reached the stable door.

"It's not quite that simple, Mr. Western. The fox was there until a few minutes ago, but I'm afraid it's not there now."

"Not here?" Sam Western's frown deepened as he stopped in his tracks. "But I thought you said . . ."

Mandy saw the color rise in Mrs. Ponsonby's cheeks. Perhaps she was regretting calling Mr. Western after all.

"It escaped." The large lady's voice faltered. "In any case, I'm still not one hundred percent sure that I want to have it destroyed."

Mr. Western snorted and pushed at the stable door. "You prefer to have it prowling around your yard for the rest of the winter, do you?"

"Of course not. But I should have consulted with the other members of my Fox Watch program before I did anything hasty."

It was Dennis Saville's turn to grunt and dismiss her protest. "Just stand clear, Mrs. Ponsonby. Let us check for his scent and see if we can pick up his trail."

"*Her* trail!" Mandy said, glaring at the two men. "You *shot* the dog fox, remember!"

As the door swung open on the empty stable, Mr. Western glanced at her. "I don't suppose you and your friend here could have had anything to do with this so-called 'escape'?"

Mandy's chin went up. She stood shoulder to shoulder with James.

"Oh, never mind," Western grunted. "Come on, Dennis, the sooner we get after this fox the better."

With Mrs. Ponsonby fussing behind them, and

Mandy's dad talking quietly to the Dixons, Mandy and James watched the landowner and his farm manager shove their way into the gloomy stable. "Let's hope we gave her a good enough start," James whispered.

Mandy nodded. "She's clever. She'd cover her tracks." She remembered what her dad had said about the wiliness of foxes.

But still they held their breaths and waited, listening to the two men poking at the straw inside the stable and muttering to each other.

"It's no good looking in there!" a voice said, loud and clear.

Mandy turned to see Sophie Dixon standing right behind them.

At the sound of her voice, Mr. Western came out. He brushed straw from his jacket, then shouldered his gun. "What's that?"

"I said it's no good looking for the fox in there. You won't find her." Sophie spoke as if she knew something important, in that secretive way she had, ignoring Mandy and James and staring at Mr. Western.

"Have you got a better idea?" he demanded.

Sophie nodded. She stood with her hands in her pockets, in her mud-covered jeans, determined to have her say. "I saw which way she went."

Mandy narrowed her eyes. *Don't you dare!* She put all her strength of will into defying Sophie. But it made no difference.

"Good. That's more like it." Western called Saville out of the stable. "This girl's got the information we need."

"How? When?" James challenged. "You weren't here!"

"That's right. Don't listen to her!" Mandy agreed. How could Sophie Dixon do this to a poor defenseless creature?

"I didn't have to be," she sneered. "I didn't see her here, did I? I saw her in the village!"

Mandy could have strangled her. She felt her face go hot with anger and then cold with dismay. For the second time in two days Sophie had betrayed their fox.

"Whereabouts?" Immediately Western took up the clue. "Where exactly did you see her?" He gestured at Saville to go ahead and start up the car engine.

"I was at the bus stop by the post office. The fox was sneaking along the back of those little houses next to the pub."

"That's Ernie Bell's place. Which way was it heading?"

Sophie narrowed her eyes. She shot a look at Mandy, warning her not to interfere.

Mandy picked up the look. Somehow it wasn't the

expression an enemy would give. *Keep quiet!* it signaled. *Trust me!*

"Which way?" Mr. Western demanded again.

"Toward the village hall."

"Crossing the main road?" For a second he looked doubtful. "In broad daylight?"

"Yes, but then it cut back behind the houses and went into the pub yard. Behind that high wall."

"Then what?" He squeezed every drop of information he could out of his willing helper.

"Then the bus came, so I don't know where it went after that. But I think it must have found something to eat in the garbage pails behind the pub, don't you?" She sounded eager, nodding her head in encouragement.

"Quite likely." Sam Western nodded hastily back. "That's a big help, thank you very much!"

With this, he strode across Mrs. Ponsonby's yard and into his car. He'd heard all he needed. Now it was time for action.

James waited until the car turned and set off down the drive, then he grabbed Mandy's arm. "Come on, what are we waiting for?" he cried.

The grown-ups had gone into a huddle, while the dogs trotted quietly around the yard. Mrs. Ponsonby kept tight hold of little Nipper and was anxiously discussing the recent turn of events.

"Come on, Mandy!" James insisted. "We're not going to give up now, are we?" He was all for cutting across the fields to get to the village before Mr. Western.

But Mandy stood firm. She was waiting for Sophie to say something. "That wasn't true, was it?" she murmured.

Sophie's pale face blushed. "I was afraid you two were going to ruin it!"

"How come?" James was puzzled. "Ruin what?"

"There I was, trying my best to make them believe what I was saying, and you were telling them not to believe me!"

"You mean it wasn't true?" James was flabbergasted. He watched Sam Western's car turn left out of the gates and speed toward the village. "You didn't see the fox?"

"Yes, I did." Sophie's eyes were beginning to gleam. "But not exactly where I said I did!"

"Wow!" His mouth fell open.

Mandy heaved a sigh of relief. "You sent them the wrong way?"

She nodded. "It's a good thing you picked up on what I was trying to do, Mandy."

"I wasn't sure . . ."

"No, and I wouldn't have blamed you for not trusting me, after what I've done." Again Sophie blushed. "I was just so worried about Nipper, I couldn't think straight."

"Never mind that now," Mandy spoke gently. "Listen, at least Nipper won't have to be put down if Mrs. Ponsonby has him." She glanced across at the lively discussion going on among the adults. "I know it's not perfect, but . . ."

"It's better than nothing," Sophie agreed with a sigh. "I just love that puppy so much, I don't know if I can bear to part with him!" Tears filled her eyes, and she wiped them away with the cuffs of her jacket.

"I'm sorry," Mandy whispered.

"What for? It should be me who's saying sorry to you. I've ruined things for your fox, haven't I?"

"No. I should have seen how hard it was for you. But I never stopped to think."

"None of us did," James cut in. "The thing is, Sophie, if you did see the fox and it wasn't by the pub, where was it?" Practical things suited him better than saying sorry.

For the first time they saw Sophie Dixon smile. The corner of her mouth curled and she shook her dark hair back from her face. "Where do you think?"

"Don't make us guess!" James protested.

But Mandy grinned back. "No, wait a minute." She thought of their last sight of the vixen; the leap down from the loft onto the stable floor, the flash of her white tail as she sped across the yard and around the side of the house.

"Where's the best place she'd found in the whole of Welford?" Sophie prompted.

"Here." Mandy looked around the yard at the up-turned pails, the deserted stables of Bleakfell Hall. "You don't mean . . ."

". . . she turned tail and came back home!" James finished the sentence for her.

Sophie admitted that she'd seen the fox return while she sat in the car watching everyone argue over Nipper. The fox had slunk back down the side of the house, across the yard, and into the stable.

"You mean, she's in there now?" Dr. Adam picked up the threads of the story as Mandy gave a high-speed account.

"Oh, Sophie!" Helena Dixon began to chide.

But Mandy's dad put up his hand to stop her. "No, she just saved a life. Please don't yell at her."

"But she lied." Sophie's mother was embarrassed.

"Well, maybe a white lie doesn't hurt when it's for a good cause. As a vet, I'm all for anything that protects the wildlife in the area, believe me!"

Mandy and James nodded hard, noticing Mrs. Ponsonby's head go to one side as she listened and considered his opinion.

"Oh, really, Adam? You see saving the fox as a question of protecting our natural heritage?"

"I certainly do, Amelia."

Mandy grinned at James and Sophie.

"Yes, I see your point. Conservation works. Perhaps that's the way for our Fox Watch program to look at it, too."

"Exactly!" Adam Hope winked at Mandy. "And very important work it is, too."

"Hmm. 'Save Our Foxes!' I like the sound of that."

"'Fight for Foxes!'" Andrew Dixon suggested. "We could certainly get something going in the neighborhood along those lines."

Sophie and Helena Dixon stared at him in surprise.

"We could enlist some help, too." Mr. Dixon sounded enthusiastic. "I'm sure Joe would broadcast the message tomorrow night if we were to ask him. The whole village will be there to watch him turn on the lights, won't they?"

"Excellent!" Mrs. Ponsonby squeezed Nipper and lent her weight to the new idea. "Perhaps we could even get him to introduce a new story line into *Dale End*. You know, a local widow who offers refuge to some starving foxes when a landowner runs them off his property!"

"Who knows?" Mr. Dixon disguised a smile. "We can certainly try."

"But meanwhile, back to reality," Dr. Adam reminded them. "According to Sophie, we have a fox holed up in your stable, Mrs. Pon — er, Amelia. And it seems she's chosen it as a safe den for the winter. If I tell you that she will present absolutely no threat to Toby and Pandora, we can take it you have no objections to her staying here?"

Mrs. Ponsonby drew herself up and took a deep breath. "Absolutely none at all, my dear Adam!"

So while the others went into the house to celebrate over coffee and apple pie, Dr. Adam took a piece of cooked chicken from Mrs. Ponsonby's fridge and went with Mandy and James into the stable. They wanted to reassure themselves that the fox had come to no harm after her recent adventures.

"Don't worry, foxes are talented survivors," Dr. Adam told them as they climbed the ladder to the loft. "And they're brilliant opportunists."

"Meaning what?" Mandy showed him the corner where the vixen had first chosen to hide.

"When they see a chance, they seize it. I'm not surprised that she made her way back here as soon as she could. After all, it's the warmest, driest place around." He stopped to look behind the pile of bales. "Yep, she's back all right."

Mandy listened. In the darkness, as her senses grew used to the gloomy stable, and she breathed in the musty, disused smell, she, too, could hear the soft, dog-like panting of the fox. "Give her the chicken, Dad," she whispered.

Dr. Adam laid the bait, stood back, and waited for the vixen to emerge. At last they saw the glow of her eyes, then the white of her muzzle and chest, as the scent of the chicken drew her out from behind the bales. They watched her take one low, delicate step, then another, her black paws invisible in the dim light. She kept the people fully in her sight as she came warily forward.

"She looks okay," Dr. Adam said, casting his expert eye over her rich, thick coat. "No damage done, I should say."

"Thank goodness." Mandy was smiling now, admiring the nerve of the vixen as she seized the piece of chicken and stared directly at them.

"That's your Christmas dinner," James told her.

They all grinned. "Do you want the other good news?" Dr. Adam asked.

"Yes, please." They took what they knew would be

their last view of the fox in her luxury den. After this, they must leave her in peace to fend for herself and live a natural life in the wild.

"It looks like she's pregnant. In March or April she should be having a litter of three or four healthy cubs."

Mandy sighed. "That's great!"

"Perfect!" James agreed.

Eleven

"Ladies and gentlemen, I take great pleasure in wishing you a very merry Christmas!"

Mandy watched as Joe Wortley stepped up on a platform, flicked a switch, and turned on the lights.

People cheered and clapped. The village square winked red and green, orange and blue. The Christmas tree towered above them, carols played on a loudspeaker, and the landlord of the Fox and Goose came around with big plates of free refreshments.

Ernie Bell was right at the front. "Merry Christmas, Mandy," he said with a wink, taking a piece of pie.

There was Walter, chatting with Jean. Grandma and

Grandpa stood in the middle of the crowd with Simon. And James had come with his mom and dad and Blackie, armed with his autograph book, standing in line for an autograph from the famous television star.

"By the way." Joe Wortley took up the microphone once more. "I've been asked to make a special announcement." He glanced down at Mrs. Ponsonby, who stood by the platform, beaming up at him. "This is on behalf of Amelia Ponsonby, who would like to invite you all to a party at Bleakfell Hall on the day after Christmas.

"As you know, Amelia has just set up a new conservation group called Fox Watch, dedicated to the protection of one of our finest local inhabitants, *Vulpes vulpes*, or the European Red Fox. The party is a fundraising effort to support her group, and, of course, refreshments of a seasonal nature will be provided. She very much hopes you'll all come!"

"Will you be there, Joe?" someone called from the crowd.

The actor nodded. "You bet," he said, before putting down the microphone.

"Then we'll be there, too," the voice promised.

Mandy stood between her mom and dad, grinning as Mrs. Ponsonby swamped Joe Wortley with thanks. Dressed for the occasion in her red coat and matching red Santa Claus hat, with Toby and Pandora at her feet, she radiated happiness.

"It's good that Sam Western's not here to hear that," Dr. Adam said quietly. There'd been no news of the landowner since Sophie had sent him off on the wild-goose chase.

"Yes, but where's Nipper?" Mandy looked hard for him between the feet of the crowd surrounding Mrs. Ponsonby and Joe Wortley. There was no sign of the puppy, yet Mandy couldn't imagine that his doting new owner would have left him behind.

"Here," a voice said from behind.

Mandy turned. "Sophie!"

"Yap!" Nipper greeted her from the safety of Sophie's arms.

"Woof!" Henrietta wasn't to be outdone. Her deep bark startled people nearby. She stared up at Mandy.

"But . . . !" Mandy looked from Sophie to Nipper to Henrietta. She glanced across at Mrs. Ponsonby's red hat bobbing through the crowd toward them.

"Mom and Dad decided we could keep Nipper after all!" Sophie declared. "Your dad helped to persuade them, Mandy. Thanks to him, Nipper can stay at the vic-arage with Henrietta and me!"

"That's fantastic!" Mandy knew that Sophie deserved it. She would love him and care for him in a special way.

"Will you come and take them for walks with me?" Sophie asked shyly. "You could help me to train Nipper if you like."

"I'd love to!" Mandy was thrilled at how well everything had turned out. But Mrs. Ponsonby was getting dangerously close. "Listen, Sophie, I'll see you later, okay? I want to tell James your good news!"

She escaped in the nick of time, just before Mrs. Ponsonby descended on Nipper.

"How's the sweet little darling?" Mandy heard the cooing voice rise above the carols. "Has he missed me, then? I'm sure he has. But he's in a very good home, so there's no need to worry his sweet little head about anything. And he's going to have such a happy Christmas, I know he is!"

"Hey!" James cried as Mandy seized his arm. "Where are we off to now?"

She pulled him away from the refreshments and the singing, out of the laughing crowd.

"Escaping from Mrs. Ponsonby," she told him. "Let's make a quick getaway!"

The frosty air nipped their faces and made their fingers and toes tingle as they circled around the back of the pub into the quiet of the fields and the dark hillside beyond. Mandy breathed in deeply and gazed up at the

clear starlit sky. A full moon cast a silvery light on the frozen landscape.

"Look there!" James whispered, pointing up the hill to a clump of hawthorn bushes, outlined in black by the light of the moon.

All was still and silent. Then Mandy saw a movement. A lonely figure the size of a smallish dog loped through the trees onto the empty moor.

But it was no dog. The nose was too sharp, the ears too pointed. And though they could only see the silhouette, the long, bushy tail gave her away.

"It's our fox," James said.

It was true, it could have been any fox setting out on its nightly excursion across the frost-covered hill. But in her heart, Mandy knew her; the low, lithe run, the silent tread.

"*Our* fox," she repeated, watching with a low satisfied sigh as the fox finally melted into the dark.